GET TO
th
TANGO PIONEERS

Myths and the Melting Pot

(Origins to 1909)

David Thomas

TANGO JOURNEY

Editor: Marion Greenwood
Published by Tango Journey
ISBN: 978-0-9955344-2-1

Thanks and Acknowledgements

First of all to Marion who has supported, and tolerated, me in my decade-long submersion in often abstruse archive material. I am grateful for her guidance in the construction and flow of the book and for her advice that not everything that is known needs to be included.

To the Archivo General de la Nación de Argentina, the Nacional Library of Spain, and the Iberian American Institute in Berlin for their mesmerising collections of publications and photographs that have brought to life my own understanding of tango history.

To the Instituto Argentino del Tango, Buenos Aires and all of its dedicated expert lecturers and the knowledgeable fellow participants on the course *Diplomatura del Historia del Tango* (2021/22)

To the many tango researchers from across the world and across the centuries whose work has fascinated and puzzled me in equal measure.

To all in the tango scene, past and present, who have added to the magic.

And finally, to you, for choosing to get to know the Tango Pioneers. I hope that you enjoy the journey.

CONTENTS

PART ONE

The Series

Myths and the Melting Pot (Origins to 1909)
Celebration of Tango Argentino (1910 to 1919)
The Precarious Years (1920 to 1935)

There are many fans of tango around the world that love to listen and dance to the music recorded from the 1930s to the 1950s, being the years that provide most of the danceable tangos played at today's *milongas* (dance events). The recorded orchestras are known by the name of the leader, or director, and so the mention of the name Francisco Canaro conjures up a particular sound, as does Carlos Di Sarli, Osvaldo Pugliese and so on[1]. Today the recordings by these maestros inspire people to dance and for that they deserve our admiration and thanks but they were simply part of a process that had begun long before they were born. As fortunate beneficiaries of those that had come before they were standing tall on the shoulders of the pioneer giants.

In this tango trilogy I introduce the pioneer performers (those that created the music) and the pioneer promoters (those that created the environment in which the later, better known, tango orchestras could thrive). We owe these tango pioneers a great deal and the intention of these books is to give them the recognition and heart-felt gratitude that they deserve.

---

[1] For more details on the orchestra leaders, musicians, and singers see the book *Get To Know Twenty Tango Orchestras*.

Read, Listen, and Watch

Throughout this book you will see two icons:  and  indicating that I have produced music and film clips for you on the linked YouTube Channel *Get To Know Tango*. Alongside the icon is a QR code - simply scan with your mobile phone and you will be taken directly to the film. I recommend that you read with on-line access so that you can enjoy the full multi-media experience of reading, listening, and watching[2].

Find out more on the website: *www.tango-journey.com*

Unfamiliar Words

If you are not from the Spanish-speaking world then there may be words used in this series that are unfamiliar to you. I have included a list with descriptions on page 175.

Sources

The research and writing of this series has been both stimulating and frustrating in equal measure, presenting me with a myriad of choices and raising questions about what is a history, what is a fact, and what is a fair perspective. The dictionary defines history as a continuous chronological record of important events, but there is more to it. There needs to be evidence, ideally in the physical form of documents, photographs, recordings, or artefacts whilst at the same time realising that the lack of hard evidence does not prove that an event did not happen.

---

[2] At time of publication all videos were available in all regions. It is possible that YouTube may change its policy on regional or copyright access. You should be able to locate the material via other on-line sources.

Much of the primary source material for the series *Get To Know the Tango Pioneers* is drawn from newspapers and magazines that reached hundreds of thousands of readers. For example, the first Buenos Aires edition of the popular Montevideo magazine *Caras y Caretas* was published on 19 August 1898 and by the end of 1907 it had a circulation of over 100,000. The content was aimed at a broad range of societal interests from politics at home and abroad, family articles, children's cartoons, sport, high and low culture, and of course many advertisements that perhaps gave the best insight in to everyday life in the city at that time. They are fascinating as a source of historical information but I have found it particularly interesting to read them as if it were the day of publication and I was idly browsing through them at the breakfast table. In that way I can better understand how (often indirect) references to tango infiltrated the public consciousness, generated interest (whether positive or negative), and thereby promoted the emerging genre.

An excellent example of the use of tango in everyday news coverage can be seen on 20 July 1912 when *Caras y Caretas* chose as its front page (of a 148-page issue) a political cartoon in full colour. The customer asks 'Give me the most fashionable record' and the retailer proffers a tango record *No Hay Plata* (There is No Money) saying 'Take this one, nothing else is heard'. The political message was clear - the caricature of the politician was saying that there were no public funds available. The imagery chosen by the cartoonist was the most popular fashion - buying tango records.

For those tango researchers who are unable to spend many months at the Buenos Aires Archivo General de la Nación de Argentina then an impressive array of relevant Spanish language publications can be found online at the Nacional Library of Spain and the Iberian American Institute in Berlin. Details of cylinder and disc recordings can be found at various sites but your first visit should be to the Discography of American Historical Recordings (hosted at https://adp.library.ucsb.edu). There are many other general publications to be found online that have very little to say specifically about Argentine tango nor its recording artists but do nevertheless provide interesting insight not provided anywhere else. For example, on 15 January 1905 a new monthly trade magazine was first published in North America called *The Talking Machine World* aimed at the already booming industry of 'the makers and sellers of talking machines'. Amongst their pages lie references to the Buenos Aires appetite for local recording artists and information about volume of sales. On-line sources such as genealogy websites, ships' passenger lists, and personal diaries all add vital confirmatory detail without any specific references to tango.

In reality, prior to the mid-20th century most people's daily lives were happily spent without leaving any tangible record therefore the remaining source to historians is oral communication, the telling of repeated tales through the generations. I have collected personal biographical detail from other people's interviews of the pioneers taken over the course of a hundred years or more.

However it is inevitable that human memory is subject to unintended inaccuracies. I have only included personal memories when they make sense in the context of the available hard evidence of documents, recordings, and photographs.

After nearly a decade of research, corroboration, analysis, interpretation, drafting and revision I can only hope that you find the series *Get To Know the Tango Pioneers* to be cogent, interesting, and entertaining.

The Tango Lens

During the long period covered by this book the people of Argentina were affected by momentous political events involving violent unrest, economic booms and busts, and the hard won granting of progressive rights and freedoms. They created, worked in, and relied upon all of the trades, professions, and infrastructure necessary to service a modern nation. They were lifted by the wide range of creativity in architecture, poetry and literature, theatre, comedy, sport, and world music. Above all of that they were concerned with their own personal aspirations, challenges, loves, and anxieties. Those of us who are interested in the history of tango (its music, dance, and people) have a tendency to view life in Buenos Aires through a special tango lens. Yet if we were able to travel back in time to interview a wide range of the population about tango we would find that some were for it, others against, but most would not have been interested enough to have had an opinion.

Over many recent decades the unguarded use of the tango lens has produced a simplistic viewpoint of history that, although easier to tell, is at best inadequate and at worst entirely misleading. During the research period for this book I had not intended to undermine my own understanding of the origins and development of tango but the compilation, comparison and contrast of a vast array of sources has led me to re-assess many assumptions that I had previously made and to file them away under 'Myths, Misunderstandings, and Muddles'.

If I were permitted to create my own description, I would say that the widely accepted history of tango is in fact a muddled mythunderstanding.

PART TWO

Myths, Misunderstandings, & Muddles

The Ancestor, Golden Age, Upper-class Rejection, Parisian Influence, Brothels, Prohibited Dance, Men Dancing with Men, Red Rose, Illiterate Musicians

1. The Ancestor

The misunderstanding here is that there is an evolutionary line from the time when the word *tango* emerged to the word *tango* that we recognise today. The so-called evolution of tango is the subject of many books, academic papers, articles, and blogs and there are seemingly endless variations of threads and false trails to explore. Most are factually accurate in part, thought-provoking, interesting and entertaining but they create a number of common misunderstandings:

1) That tango is tango is tango. There is often no clarity about what aspect of tango is being referred to: is it the music, the dance, or the lyrics? The tango with which we are most familiar today did not originate and develop as a fixed package of music, dance, and lyrics. Each of those three elements had its own variety of influences, its own direction, and its own pace of development.

2) That tango is tango is tango. Many authors point to the earliest appearance of the word 'tango' and lay claim to that being the 'source'. It is interesting that the appearance of the word 'tango' (and close variations of it) across the continents of Africa, Europe, and the Americas is nearly always linked to dance, music, and meeting venues. However the connection with the use of the word 'tango' that emerged in Buenos Aires at the start of the 1900s is either remote or completely disconnected. A few examples:

- in old Spanish & Portuguese (the main linguistic influencers in the Americas) the first person singular conjugation of the verbs *tangir* and *tanger* (meaning to touch, chime, pluck, and drum) produces the sound 'tango', more or less;
- the Etymological Dictionary of Spanish places tango as a dance form introduced by the Portuguese in to the

Canary Islands[3] long before the colonial adventures to the Americas;

- across the Atlantic the Quechan language has *tambo* meaning a shelter for milking cows that over the years came to be a rustic meeting place. It eventually entered Buenos Aires terminology as a dance space for the black Argentinians and became interchanged with the word tango;
- from 1802 there are written references to tango dance halls as Casas de Tango, Tango de Bayle[4], Bayles de Tambo;
- the word Tango appears in the 1836 Cuban dictionary[5] defined as a meeting place for negros to dance to the sound of their drums.

What can we make of it all? Only that we need to be careful before we jump to conclusions that historic references to tango form part of the ancestry of the *tango argentino* familiar today.

3) That tango is the product of genetic/racial properties.
In the search for the tango ancestor there are many claims of originating ownership. Some convincingly demonstrate tango (music and dance) to have African origins, others are equally successful in their assertions that the origins are European, mainly Italian.

Let us look briefly at some of the evidence linking those of African descent to tango. The subject leads to a debate charged with great sensitivity: those who dispute African origins are said to be attempting to erase black history from tango replacing it with an entirely white European origin. Those that pursue the African

---

[3] still today danced as tango herreño

[4] bayle or baile means dance

[5] Diccionario Provincial de Voces Cubanas (1836)

linkage are said to be pursing an ideological agenda, a socio-cultural re-balance. Each has a tendency to exaggerate in order to press home their viewpoint until there are two uncompromising positions. Reality of course is neither black nor white. Example evidence includes:

- the places named Tango in Mali and in Angola. Despite some repeated claims to the contrary place names are not evidence of the origin of tango, whether music or dance;
- in May 1822 (and again in December 1831) the *Diario de Madrid* announced a play at the Teatro de la Cruz that included a dance entitled 'the Tango of the Negros'. There is nothing more known about the music or the dance but my guess is that it was drum-based and involved participants dancing solo and not in an embrace;
- on 11 July 1869 the regular Sunday afternoon bullfight in the city of Lisbon involved a small group of young black men 'dancing a tango'. Again the tango movements are not described in any of the reports but I can imagine that they were danced solo and energetically to excite both the crowds and the bulls;
- in March 1886 the book *Memories of the War of Paraguay* described a group of musicians three quarters of whom were of African descent and they played a 'tango quebrada that only the Brazilians knew how to dance'. It is an intriguing line but disappointingly no more light can be thrown on either the music or the dance. In the early 1900s the Brazilian maxixe was widely described as tango in South America and in Europe;
- the Madrid magazine *La Moda Elegante* (January 1890) described several popular dances and in one line loaded with images of sensuality said 'we owe to Cuba the tango, the dance of negros …… that, like the *habanera*, has the voluptuousness of that region's climate'. In Spain at that time tango was energetic and often danced solo like

flamenco and so the reason for thanking Cuba for the voluptuous 'tango of negros' is a mystery;

- the front covers of sheet music printed from the 1840s to 1900s for tango americano/tango habanera often depicted images of scantily clad black natives of some fictional land. The music was always composed by Europeans, the illustrations drawn by Europeans, the sheet music printed by Europeans, and the music played by Europeans. The association of tango to an exotic image was a marketing ploy not dissimilar to the portrayal of 1920s/1930s tango orchestras from the sophisticated city of Buenos Aires as countryside *gauchos*. We can only hope that in centuries to come future tango researchers do not argue, supported by photographic evidence, that tango was undoubtedly a musical form of the gauchos.

It is important to differentiate between black-skinned and African. It is clear from the above examples that black-skinned people in the Iberian Peninsula, South America, and the Caribbean danced something described as tango but we do not know the form of that dance, nor whether it was one or completely different types of dance, nor do we know the accompanying music in most of those cases. Ethnomusicologists (experts in music history) can find no linkage between music from African countries and the 20th century tango of the Río de la Plata. Ethnochoreologists (experts in dance history) can detect some common or at least similar movements, mainly bent knees, with the black-skinned dance styles and 'modern' tango. In my inexpert view those dance similarities could also be coincidental as there are only so many comfortable movements a human body can make.

To further support the African heritage of tango many commentators point to the black-skinned composers and musicians like Rosendo Mendizábal, Carlos Posadas, Gabino

Ezeiza, even to the relatively modern Horacio Salgán (who died in 2016). I say that their creativity came from their environment in Argentina not from some gene inherited from a distant ancestor born in Africa. We should also be cautious about the portrayal of the Afro-Argentinian as a lower-class, drum-beating, carnival-goer acting out some inner-African tango. There were many highly respected black leaders in business, the church, the intellectual arts and all of the skilled trades of the city and so apart from skin colour their association with Africa was long past. Many authors are also too quick to link black-skinned tango pioneers from the 1880s onwards with the word slavery. It is worth noting that in Argentina slavery was abolished in 1853, preceding North America by a decade, and much earlier in 1813 a law had already declared that no child should be born in to slavery - therefore the children of slaves were free citizens.

So if we cannot point to the African influences where else can we look? Domingo Faustino Sarmiento (Argentina President 1868 to 1874) described his country as a melting pot, 'a mixture of the wealthy rural cities like Córdoba and their pure descendants of the Spanish colonialists; towns like Santiago del Estero with the native Indians that speak the Quechan dialect; Buenos Aires that is full of foreigners[6]; and of course the last remnants of the Argentine negro'. Let's quickly look at the colonialists and the aboriginal people. From the 1500s a series of incursions and settlements by European adventurers culminated in a Spanish cultural dominance for the next 300 years. All of those arrivals, across the centuries from the 1600s to 1800s, brought with them their own forms of music and dance that mixed with those of the native Americans. Entries in diaries and letters from the earliest European settlers confirm unsurprisingly that the aborigine peoples of the Americas played instruments (horns and drums),

[6] meaning recent European immigrants

sang songs (from lively to melancholic), and danced (through the night fortified by alcohol).

Ethnomusicologists have established links from the aborigine tribes to many of today's folkloric rhythms such as the nostalgic love songs of yaraví, the triste, chamamé, and the tonada cuyana. I am not suggesting that tango is derived from aboriginal song but do assert that there were many ingredients in the melting pot (that has been stirred many times) and although their individual flavours may now be indiscernible nothing was wasted. Without them the overall taste today would certainly be different. The tango pioneer Vicente Greco's sheet music for his tango *El Estribo* was marked 'inspired by a vidalita'. The vidalita melody has been detected in the tangos *Qué Noche* by Agustín Bardi and others by Eduardo Arolas, Roberto Firpo, and Francisco Canaro. In 1916 Carlos Gardel recorded as an estilo *El Moro,* a gaucho song from the mid-1800s, and the following year Roberto Firpo recorded it as a tango for the dance hall. In the mid-20th century the tango orchestra leader Aníbal Troilo recognised the link between folk music and tango when he asked Antonio Rodríguez Villar, the president of the Academia Nacional de Folklore, to sing for him a country milonga, estilo, cifra, or cielito. Troilo said that in order to be a good tango singer one had to know how to sing an estilo. The folkloric genre was and is the heart of Argentinian music and so it was inevitable that its influence would contribute to tango in the 20th century. The tango pioneers from the 1890s to the 1920s all performed (and many recorded) those folk tunes that became known simply as *musica criolla* a form initially indiscernible from that which became known as tango.

My conclusions are that:

- the influences that created the tango music and dance of Argentina from the 1880s came from the local environment and not from some mysterious inherited musical chromosomes lying deep within any racial or national group;

- we cannot assume an association between everything that was once labelled tango; and
- there was no single ancestor, nor discernible evolutionary line.

2. The Golden Age

The phrase Golden Age of tango, or *La Epoca de Oro*, is now a cliché and is widely considered to be somewhere between 1935 and 1955, with some opinions narrowing it down further to the 1940s. The Golden Age accolade was given (many years after the event) based on the proliferation of orchestras filling dance halls, broadcasting on the radio, making records, and featuring in films. I do not dispute the title but it creates the myth that tango was slowly evolving until it reached its peak interest during those years. The effect is to distort the history of tango and to diminish earlier, equally exciting, Golden Ages. Similarly, the years between 1935 and 1955 often attract today the label of 'traditional' in relation to the era's music, dance, and social behaviour at milongas. Again that is all perfectly fine if it is also known and acknowledged that there were different tango traditions long before the so-called traditional.

One could argue that the first Golden Age of tango was somewhere between the 1880s and 1900 as its demise was noted in the magazine *Caras y Caretas* on 7 February 1903: 'the famous cultivators of tango and their music have disappeared from the stage. If we do not do anything about it we will hear the funeral bells announce its death'. In 1903 tango fans were witnessing not only the end of their Golden Age but the complete demise of tango music, dance, and culture as they knew it. To the modern tango fan this may be an astonishing observation that in 1903 tango music and dance was considered to be on the brink of extinction, especially as most of the recordings that are heard in today's milongas were made some 30 to 50 years after that date. The 1903 article was concerned about the dying of the fun-filled, energetically danced, and politically tribal tango that came from the music and dances of the milonga, gato, pericon, and cueca. In the article, the journalist hoped that the theatre company of the Podestá brothers would take that traditional tango to Paris in order to re-energise it back home so that once again there would be men in country attire with ponchos around their shoulders and red carnations behind their ears (symbolising their political allegiance), leading quebradas so that their women with daggers in their garters (that they were quick to use) were turned so far backwards that their cheeks would almost be brushing the ground. If action was not taken quickly, he said, then tango would be lost to the present-day common city folk who were bastardising the traditional dances in to a poor copy of the African candombe and lazily sliding in to the slow habanera, practicing in their conventillo yards to the sound of a street organito. Today's tango reader will view the latter description as the accepted origins of tango but at the time it apparently signalled not the start but the end of tango. The article identified changes in the style of tango that had not suddenly happened but had been developing over the course of years.

The 19th century writer Ventura Lynch is credited with first identifying the genre of Argentinian folk music and dance *(folklorico)* and then linking those traditions with the emerging scene in the city of Buenos Aires. In 1883 he wrote that the music known as milonga, that resembled the song of the gaucho payadors, had become the sound of the common people in both the provinces and the city. I paraphrase: 'The milonga is so universal in the environs of the city that it is an obligatory piece at all of the lower-class dances and it is now heard on guitars, on paper-combs, and from the itinerant musicians with their flutes, harps[7] and violins. It has also been taken up by the organ-grinders, who have arranged it to sound like the habanera dance. It is danced too in the low life clubs around the main markets, and also at the dances of cart-drivers, soldiers, and compadres and compadritos'. Several decades later Jorge Luis Borges, in his many poetic works on the subject of tango, held similar views that the good old days of 'brave and manly' tango with its political stabbings and fights were ruined later by the immigrants, the bandoneón, the contrived use of lunfardo, and effeminate lyrics.

The last few years covered by this book saw the early dawning of the next Golden Age that would truly start after 1910 with the celebration of the bandoneonists and the orquesta típica (that initially was anything from a trio to a sextet).

Before we continue with the next myth I will add a word about another muddle: the categorisations known as *Guardia Vieja* and *Guardia Nueva*. They are terms in common use but not with common meaning. Usually they are applied:

- to dates, *Vieja* is nominally before 1917/1920 (and sometimes applied up to 1930) or;
- to simple music without arrangement (but sometimes to any recording that just sounds old and scratchy).

The date and style delineation takes no account of sophisticated compositions and arrangements evident on tango recordings from 1914. The terms were invented with good intention to try to bring some kind of order and definition but they do not work, they do not make sense, and they lead to more misconceptions, misunderstandings, and muddles. It is best to be aware of the terms but to avoid their use.

---

[7] a harp conjures up an image of refinement but was a common gaucho instrument in the Americas

3. Upper Class Rejection

The myth is that the aristocracy is said to have rejected the music, dance, and song of tango. There is some supporting evidence to show that there were individuals within the upper classes who vociferously rejected tango. However, there is continuous and widespread evidence demonstrating that the so-called decent society was clearly enjoying tango (as both music and dance) in cafés, carnivals, and the theatres; buying tango sheet music to play on their pianos at home; listening to the first tango records on the newly imported gramophones; and having lessons to teach them the latest tango dance.

As well as being consumers of tango it was the middle and higher classes of society that produced many of the early composers, musicians, and dancers. As far back as 30 August 1866 the newspaper *La Tribuna* referenced a tango called *La Coqueta* (the flirting woman) that was dedicated to the conservative Society of Buenos Aires. Also in 1866 the classically trained cathedral organist José María Palazuelos composed a 'tango habanera' *El Negro Schicoba* that was performed at the theatre during the following year's carnival season.

In 1880 the Spanish classically trained musician, Gabriel Diez, composed a tango inspired by the locals of Buenos Aires (where he had lived since 1870) and called it *El porteñito*[8].

On 9 March 1900 the newspaper *La Nación* reported a dance held on the pavement outside of a city hospital. It was

[8] not the same as the later one, familiar today, composed by Ángel Villoldo

organised and attended by the young medical staff who, it is safe to say, were not from the lower classes of Buenos Aires society. They had hired a street organ and danced the 'best milongas and tangos', an indication that (despite being two years before the first disc recorded in Argentina) there was already a sense of a large and well-known tango repertoire. The journalist was shocked at the behaviour and called it shameful (evidence of the establishment's rejection) but the fact remains that the event was held and enjoyed, openly and publicly, by representatives of the middle and upper classes. And so the reality of the alleged split between upper and lower classes was more a case of individual snobbery. Some liked it, some did not, and some had no opinion.

4. Parisian Influence

The myth is that the Buenos Aires high society only accepted tango once it had gained frenzied popularity amongst the Parisian *haute monde* after 1910. This has some truth in the case of those individuals who caught on late but there were already many in high society who were enthusiastic about tango prior to the Paris craze.

- Miguel Tornquist was born in 1873 to an aristocratic family and led a bohemian and short life. He composed several tangos, the sheet music of which was published in the newspapers for readers to be able to play at home. One in 1904, *El Batarás*, was described as a tango *criollo* and dedicated to his friend Belisario Roldán junior[9] - a tango criollo dedicated by one upper class man to another in 1904. It is a pity that Tornquist did not make

[9] the son of the influential politician and author

any recordings because his style was interesting. He constantly improvised, never played the same tune in the same way twice, and his right hand created smooth melodies whilst his left hammered the bass notes. The playwright, theatre and silent film director, Enrique García Velloso, described him as having the merry incoherence of a madman blending together tangos, country milongas, vidalas, gatos and other rhythms. During the year of his early death in 1908 he composed *Tango histerico* and dedicated it to the founder of the Argentinian Psychological Society.

There were others that were not only tango converts but who took it to Paris and influenced European high society, rather than the other way around:

- Alberto López Buchardo (born in Buenos Aires in 1882) abandoned his studies at the Faculty of Medicine and accepted his parents offer to pay for him to follow his artistic heart to Paris. He was already smitten by tango and so in Paris in 1903 he was asked to play tangos on the piano and to teach the dance (encouraged by the European assumption that, being Argentinian, he must have known what he was doing). His influence grew and he composed several tangos including two still known to us today:
    - *Germaine* recorded by Carlos Di Sarli (1941, 1951, and 1955); and
    - *Entre dos fuegos* recorded by Juan D'Arienzo (1940).

- Daniel Maximilano Videla Dorna Duportal (born in 1887) was a rebellious teenager and in about 1903 had somehow discovered tango music and, despite his privileged aristocratic upbringing, became well-known as a dancer in the less salubrious tango venues. He travelled to Paris in about 1905 where he danced and promoted tango.

- Ricardo Güiraldes was born in 1886 in to a wealthy family and spent his childhood moving between their country estate, their Buenos Aires home, and their business interests in Europe. A letter to his aunt when he was 8 years old tells us that he was already playing milongas and tangos on his guitar. He started dancing tango in his late teens and travelled with his friend Daniel Dorna in about 1905 to Paris, where he spent much of his short life until he died in 1927. Whilst there he became famous as a tango dancer and performed at the renowned Madame Rezke's dance hall.

Once the Parisian tango craze was established it did of course spread, rather than create, the popularity of tango amongst the elite in Buenos Aires.

5. The Brothels

The most ubiquitous myth is that tango was born in the brothels of Buenos Aires. That particular seedy image is depicted in stage shows, films, and novels influencing the wider public's opinion of the music and the dance. Disappointingly the exaggerated role of the brothel is also commonly found in non-fiction history books. There are four main reasons to explain why so much has been written about brothels and tango:

1) it makes a good story, hence the continuing images and storylines in anything related to tango;

2) a misunderstanding of everyday life at that time. Many street cafés offering music and stage shows were licensed to have law-abiding prostitutes serving drinks, dancing, and (if required) rooms were available upstairs or at an adjoining hotel. The cafés were open to the street, as they are today, and most customers (both men and women) were there for the main purpose of drinking, eating, enjoying the entertainment and socialising, and not interested in 'taking a room'. Public premises like this have been described over the decades as brothels which may be technically correct in part but gives the modern reader a misleading image;

3) tango lyrics are often said to have sexual innuendo that reflect the context of tango life in brothels. I find this repeated association to be unfounded and tiresome. The vast majority of tangos did not have suggestive titles. The vast majority of tangos when composed did not have any lyrics. The pioneer musicians (that we will meet in Part Four) performed only instrumental tangos. Tangos for dancing were instrumental. Tangos played in the street on organitos and wandering musicians were not accompanied by singers. Tangos played at large gatherings like carnivals did not have singers because without microphones and amplification they could not have

been heard. It is not at all clear when nor where these lyrics would have been sung, nor by who nor for whom. It is clear that tangos in theatres were sung and often the words were published that show us that in general they were simply extensions of the play's storyline, often intended to make the audience laugh, and sometimes naughty but never obscene. So that leaves us with the single guitarist/singer in small café-bars who could have included spicy lyrics - hardly the defining genre of tango. So let us turn to the few tango lyrics that contain sexual innuendo and look at them in context. There are many examples of erotic writing in Argentinian literature and folk songs from the 1890s/1900s but none are alleged to have been spawned in the brothels. Internationally the traditional folk songs of many nations are often bawdy yet similarly are never framed in the context of brothels. In England from the middle of the 1800s music hall songs were nearly always spiced with double meaning and there are accounts of prostitutes openly working in the theatres. However no-one has ever alleged that the musical genre was born in the brothels of Victorian England;

4) brothels and tango have been linked because of the opinions of two influential figures: Enrique Laretta (the Argentinian ambassador in Paris 1910 to 1919) and Leopoldo Lugones (an Argentinian aristocrat, diplomat, politician, poet, author, journalist, playwright, and historian). In the newspaper *La Nación* (22 December 1913) an article entitled 'El tango argentino' included an interview with Laretta in Paris in which he said that 'the tango in Buenos Aires is a dance exclusive to brothels from where it has not come out except to conquer Europe'. If he truly said that then his personal view is clear although it is undermined by the facts. There does remain a possibility that the much quoted article was a satirical sketch by the journalist and that Laretta had not been interviewed. Leopoldo Lugones, on the other hand, did write

his own articles and it is clear that he was not a fan of the city's tango and wanted to encourage the 'people' (namely the lower classes) to educate themselves about fine music and poetry. He is often quoted as saying 'the object of tango is to describe the obscene…tango forms the choreography of the brothel and so when women of the 20th century dance tango they know or should know that they look like prostitutes, because this is a dance of prostitutes'. However, having read his article in *La Nación* (23 November 1913) I suspect that his viewpoint was not completely as has been reported. He had attended a conference at the Academy of Arts in Paris where the poet and dance enthusiast, Jean Richepin, was speaking about tango. Lugones was arguing against the image promoted by Paris that tango was the dance of the gauchos, savages, and negros that was converted to a modern dance by the Parisians. He was also concerned about the spread of the Parisian image that was sexualising the dance: 'there is nobody that doesn't know the obscene character of the dance…the choreography of the brothel…a pornographic show'. He concluded that 'tango is not a national dance, to accept it as ours just because it is being said in Paris, would be to fall in to servitude'. Although he knew little about tango in 1913 Buenos Aires, he was clear that he did not want Argentina's reputation to be associated with the overtly sensual image of tango that he had witnessed in Paris.

Often the referenced so-called evidence linking tango with prostitution simply does not exist. The 1887 census of Buenos Aires listed just over 600 prostitutes but history books, written a century later, misquote that same census as identifying 1000 brothels. Irrespective of the numbers, there is no evidence of tango being danced in brothels. It is correct that in 1883 one brothel was closed for a week because of unlicenced dancing during the afternoon at a birthday party, but there was no mention of tango. To support the story of tango as a debauched activity linked with prostitution it is often alleged that the Roman Catholic Pope Pius X (from 1903 to 1914) issued a decree to prohibit the dance. Diligent historians during the 1960s made extensive searches and confirmed that no such pronouncements were ever made, not even those that could be misunderstood as such.

A more recent contributor to the myth is the celebrated and still revered poet, author, and philosopher Jorge Luis Borges. He was not a historian but intended, with his poetic style, to create national and cultural myths in support of the heroic gauchos and their songs. His own lifestyle was far removed from the national identity he tried to forge. Jorge Francisco Isidoro Luis Borges Acevedo was born in 1899, a descendant of military leaders and son of a lawyer, and at the age of 15 he moved to Geneva and stayed in Europe until 1921. His views on the development of urban tango were generally negative because urban life contrasted with his romanticised view of the noble countryside gaucho. As a result he was only too keen to support the disparaging myth that tango came from the brothels. His literary standing remains such that later serious writers mistakenly use his poems as historical fact. In 2001 the publication *The Economist*, in its background to a financial crisis in Argentina, boldly said that tango grew from the brothels of Buenos Aires.

So from where did tango emerge if not from brothels? From the 1880s, newspaper articles and personal recollections often mentioned gatherings in conventillos where tango and other rhythms were played and danced; similarly at carnivals, theatres, the silent cinemas, in cafés, shops, and public parks. In fact in most places where ordinary citizens participated openly and lawfully in their leisure time. A detailed account of Buenos Aires in the 1830s (published in 1881) noted that many of the barbers were black, highly sociable, and nearly all of them were guitarists, suggesting that music was played for the men that gathered. There was no mention of tango but if we look closer at the performing history of the tango pioneers then we will notice that Juan Maglio, Genaro Espósito, and Manuel Pizarro regularly played their bandoneóns to entertain the customers at barbershops. Sebastián Piana (creator of the milonga dance genre in 1932) recalled that his father was a barber and played tangos for his customers on his mandolin. Victor Lomuto, the father of the future orchestra leader Francisco, also played tangos on his violin at a barbershop. The 1915 play *Peluguería y Cigarreria* (Hairdresser and Tobaconnist) centred on a payador playing guitar and singing in a barbershop. In the 1920s bandoneón pioneer Domingo Santa Cruz played in a tango quartet every day at a barbershop in the city centre street of Corrientes[10] and even broadcast on Radio Belgrano as 'the barbershop boys'. Yet there is no suggestion that tango was born in the barbershops of Buenos Aires despite the appealing alliteration.

In the 1870s Nemesio Trejo (right), who later became a payador and playwright of tango scenes, learnt to play guitar at a general store called La Milonga. On 16 May 1892 the magazine *El Cascabel* mentioned a guitarist in a general store who played a well-known tanguito (a familiar term for a tango). Many other pioneers such as Agustín Bardi, Genaro Espósito, and Samuel Castriota performed in general stores and yet there is no suggestion that tango was born in the corner shops of Buenos Aires.

It is safe to conclude that, yes, tango was played and danced in places where sex was also traded but not as often nor by as many people as it was nearly everywhere else. The relationship between

[10] today's wider Avenida Corrientes was not created until 1936

tango and brothels is somewhere between insignificant and non-existent.

6. The Prohibited Dance

The myth is that the dance of tango was so lascivious due to its uniquely close, intimate embrace that it and the music that provoked it were, on numerous occasions, prohibited. The truth is that tango was not always in an embrace and when it was it was certainly not unique.

Tango was not always in an embrace

- in France in 1854 the dance teacher Maurice Mayer (under the pseudonym of Markowski) published a description of the steps of a new European ballroom dance called 'Le Tango' that involved no more than the touching of extended hands. The sheet music (composed by a prolific French composer Traugott-Benjamin Missler) described it as a Tango Americano in 2/4 time and the front cover showed a European couple dancing apart, with fingertips touching;
- on 30 November 1882 the magazine *La Ilustración Argentina* published a drawing entitled 'El Tango' showing a black man and woman dancing face to face but completely apart;
- in the Barcelona magazine *Pluma y Lápiz* in April 1903 drawings of the dancing figures of the vals, the schotis, and the polka are all couples in a close embrace whereas the tango illustration shows a woman dancing solo in a flamenco style.

None of these of course were 'tango argentino'.

Other dances had an intimate embrace

The surprising reality is that many popular dances in the 1800s such as the vals, polka, and mazurka all involved the socially acceptable close embrace. In the absence of photographs we can refer to drawings and paintings:

- prints published in 1825 London show couples in a variety of dance positions. Both shown here are familiar as embraces in today's tango;
- paintings by Pierre-Auguste Renior show couples in France in a close embrace, just like tango but it is not: *Bal du moulin de la Galette* (1876), *La dance à Bougival*, *Danse à la ville*, and *Danse à la Campagne* (all 1883);
- on 19 December 1897 the Barcelona magazine *Álbum Salón* published an illustration of couples dancing in a close embrace. The associated short story concerned an Argentinian payador and the melancholy tones of his milonga;

- on 27 December 1902 in *Caras y Caretas* another short story was set in a yard outside an army barracks that had been turned in to a dance space where soldiers and women danced in close embrace to the habanera played on guitar. A drawing of the scene leaves no doubt that the physical closeness of the dancers is what we recognise today as the tango embrace. Habanera and tango were

sometimes confused with each other but the two dances were considered to be very different: on 8 February 1902 *El Pais* described the dance of the habanera as 'voluptuous' and that of the tango simply as 'very creole'.

Tango was a lascivious dance

In Buenos Aires we can start to track the allegations of intimate embraces and overly sexualised dancing in the 1870s, but they were not directed at tango. At the time of tango's emergence in the city the raised eyebrows were exclusively for the polka and the

habanera. On 16 January 1870 the newspaper *La República* described the 'intimate' polkas and habanera with couples dancing chest to chest, the woman's face pressed against the man's. On 28 October 1879 in *La Patria Argentina* the reporter described his visit to the Tancredi dance hall in the barrio of La Boca where the locals danced polka and contradanzas with 'almost acrobatic quebradas' - moves that involved bending the woman backwards almost to the floor. On 28 July 1884 *La Crónica* revealed its dislike of the modern 'polka pornográfica'. It seems that the critics had their sights on other apparently lascivious dances long before tango became so popular but when tango did appear they continued to use the same terms and tone[11]. In *Caras y Caretas* (21 January 1899) a drawing showed the habanera being danced to the music of two guitars at a country fiesta. The couples were described as intimately embraced with their legs brushing together, the woman's head resting on the man's shoulder and whilst he turned to the left and to the right she remained completely committed to him. The author observed that the connection was not only to each other but to the music: 'reacting to the playful pauses in the music he holds her more tightly, her palpitating chest intimately against his'. Some 20th century students of this static drawing quibble about the implied movements saying that it represents not the lazy habanera but the more energetic polka-habanera that emerged in about 1880. Either way it was not tango.

Tango was a prohibited dance

Before I get to the misunderstandings that generated this myth, I will point to evidence that the opposite was true - tango was not only widely accepted but the dancing was admired. Every February and March the press reported extensively on the annual carnival season. Carnivals were not the place for experiments with new and unfamiliar music and dance steps. The most popular genres already familiar to all, across the city and across the social classes, were played there. Therefore we can learn a lot from those reports and safely apply that knowledge to everyday dance events

---

[11] See *www.libraryofdance.org/manuals/antidance/* for over 100 European and North American publications denouncing the sins of dance from 1545 to the modern day, none of which included tango. The 1904 *Immorality of Modern Dances,* for example, was more concerned about the 'sinful square dances'. Accounts of tango as immoral must be read in the context that all dances have been denounced as such.

throughout the rest of the year[12]. There are several newspaper observations about tango being danced well, courteously, and attractively by all classes of people. During the carnival dance held at the Teatro Victoria (in February 1901) *El Pais* noted that the attending dancers were of the sort who looked like domestic staff (specifically maids, servants, cooks) and they danced well to the vals, the habanera, and particularly well to the tango. The Teatro Argentino was cheaper and attracted what *El Pais* described as the '2nd class crowd' who despite their class were noted as excellent dancers. The Teatro Pasatiempo was described as always having been the favourite of all the social classes and in February 1902 the orchestra provided good music (many tangos and milongas) and the compadritos in particular were skilled and elegant. That description deserves repeating: the compadritos were elegant - this is not the description of legend as they are supposed to have been coarse and bawdy. The following year *El Pais* again reported on the February carnival at the Teatro Victoria but that time focused on the most famous creole dancers who danced the tango of the 'pure blood characteristic' and were agile in the difficult steps. The carnival was perhaps the most hedonistic time of the year - if one were to throw oneself in to a promiscuous dance then carnival was the time and place to do it but, on the contrary, it seems that the tango dance was an attraction to be admired.

So, if tango was not unusual in its close embrace, was not danced in a sexualised way, and was socially acceptable then why does the often-repeated myth say that the tango dance was prohibited? I have selected a few examples of why this particular myth has developed.

From the mid to late 1800s there are many official police reports and newspaper articles about illegal dancing being broken up and dancers being dispersed or arrested. Those seeking details of the

---

[12] just as today, the newspapers did not tend to report on routine dance nights

origins of tango were particularly drawn to official accounts but in the absence of specific details being mentioned, like tango, then assumptions were made. It is an undisputed fact that public dancing was prohibited unless officially approved. It is not a fact that tango dancing was prohibited. On the face of it any prohibition seems shockingly harsh however today in many countries the act of playing music and dancing in cafés, bars, and community halls is also prohibited unless licensed. That situation is considered to be normal and we do not consider ourselves to be living in an era when dance is prohibited. As far as I am aware most venues that offer such entertainment today readily pay for the licence as part of the normal cost of doing business and so enforcement action is rare. In Buenos Aires in the late 1800s there was less compliance and the subsequent police action greater. In the Buenos Aires police archives there is an internal report dated 3 May 1881 from the senior officer in charge of a central city area that is a defensive excuse to explain why, given the licensing restrictions, there continued to be so many unauthorised dances, excess drinking, and resulting public disorder on the streets. His area had about 15,000 inhabitants (a third of which were in overcrowded conventillos) that increased at weekends to about 20,000. His 21 officers were under pressure. His men were faced with café owners who used bell systems to alert the revellers when there was police activity on the street. The music and dancing stopped until his men had moved on. His detailed report made no mention of tango because the type of dance and music was entirely irrelevant.

In 1880 the newspaper *La Patria Argentina* published a wonderful description of one of those unlicensed dance events in the back-room of a café. The organito[13] was completed smothered by a mattress to keep the sound from leaking out in to the street but the resulting dull bass notes were enough to keep the dancers on the

[13] a portable organ operated by turning a handle

beat. There was no mention of tango. In that café on that night there were few women and so men danced with men - this is where we collide with another myth (covered in more detail below). In 1881 *El Diario* reported on a similar dance room in a café that had equal men and women dancing to the sound of an organito but that time the music was identified: habaneras and milongas[14].

As well as unlicensed dancing in venues there were also 'pop-up' dance gatherings in the street and the courtyards of conventillos[15]. Just like today they also required a licence but the main reason for police involvement was the blocking of pavements and public disturbance, often following complaints from the surrounding residents. On 13 May 1881 the newspaper *La Pampa* reported police intervening to stop a city centre street dance because one of the girls had drawn a dagger. As usual there was no indication of the music and tango was certainly not mentioned. Another typical scenario appeared in the newspaper *El Diario* on 17 December 1896. Couples were dancing on the street to the musical accompaniment of an organito. The police arrived and broke up the party. "Is it prohibited to enjoy yourself?" asked one indignant dancer. "No" replied the policeman "but it is forbidden to dance on the pavement". He could have added that it was also prohibited to create a disturbance in a residential area after 10 in the evening. Unusually that particular reported incident did mention the music: it was not tango but polka.

I will finish with a case that did mention tango, a gunshot and an arrest. In May 1896 a group of 6 musicians were busking amongst the theatre crowds on the Calle Corrientes. Their instruments were the usual ones of guitar, violin, and flute and their repertoire included 'tanguito criollo and compadrón'. A policeman intervened because they were playing after 10 in the evening (not

---

[14] not the milonga music with which we are familiar today, devised in 1932

[15] cramped social housing

because they were playing tangos). The reason it was reported in the newspaper *El Tiempo* is because when the musicians dispersed the policeman unreasonably fired a warning shot and apprehended one who was not as fast as the other 5. It was not a story about forbidden tango. In all of the cases I have found the police interventions were due to some breach of regulations or suspected criminal offences and none were related to the type of music or the dance.

Somehow these types of incidents have been absorbed in to the tango story and then further elaborated to portray the police acting to break up tango parties. There is absolutely no evidence of that ever happening. I am sorry if that spoils the *frisson* of the tango image.

A minor but nevertheless persistent myth is the rejection/prohibition of two particular dance moves (*cortes* & *quebradas*) that were supposedly the signature moves of compadritos and women of low morals. A corte is a cut or sharply interrupted step. A quebrada is 'breaking' of the woman's axis at the hip, as if dropping her to the floor. The truth is that:

- the quebradas were first common in other dances. In 1889 Henri de Toulouse-Lautrec painted a (non-tango) dancing scene, *Moulin de la Galette*, in which a man has taken a wide sideways step and tipped over the woman at her waist. In 1894 Paul Hoeniger also produced a painting entitled *Moulin de la Galette* and in it was a couple in a quebrada posture with the woman bent backwards;
- the cortes were not only danced by the upper classes but rewarded. At a ball in February 1906 at the Teatro Casino couples judged to have danced the best cortes won a selection of 18 carat gold jewellery.

7. Men Dancing with Men

The myth is not that men frequently danced tango with other men but that they did so due to a shortage of women. The extended tale is that, during the mass immigration of almost entirely single men from countries across Europe at the end of the 19th century, a sense of isolation drove them to find ways to communicate with

each other. The men shared their music from back home as best as they could and started to invent movements in a close embrace. From that appeared a new form of music and dance that became known as tango. I was reasonably happy to accept that simple explanation but having delved in to the detail I was not too surprised to discover that men dancing with men in a close embrace was not due to scarcity of women, was not particularly linked to tango, and was not a social phenomenon of Argentina.

The suggestion that men danced with men because of the scarcity of women begins to look flawed when we look to the census data during the last decades of the 1800s and find that the gender balance was more or less equal, averaging at 53% men and 47% women. There were some isolated years when male immigration was double that of female, but the overall differential was softened by the established population and a 'normal' birth gender ratio. There is nothing in the newspapers during those decades to suggest there was any gender imbalance and photographs of the immigrant ships and of the Buenos Aires Hotel des Inmigrantes all show large numbers of women, as do the 1890 photographs of the conventillos.

Detailed contemporary accounts of Buenos Aires from the 1830s to 1890s[16] did not notice any imbalance and described a full and vibrant society with women featuring in every aspect of daily life. The myth may have been helped by a number of photographs:

- the magazine *Fray Mocho* (1912) showed couples dancing, the majority of which were men with men. The description said 'due to the lack of women the partners were formed by men only'. I wonder whether these words have at some point been extrapolated to mean a lack of women in society as a whole. It is clear to me that the author meant only at that particular dance. In the same year, in the same city, *Caras y Caretas* included a photograph of an outdoor party in La Boca at which the only couples dancing were men with women. In both cases the text does not make any mention of tango and so the photographs could have captured any of the popular dances of the day;

- on 7 February 1903 two men were photographed, dressed in working-class attire including boots, demonstrating tango steps together. It is not clear what

[16] *Recuerdos de Buenos Aires* (1897) Silverio Dominguez; *Buenos Aires Setenta Años Atrás* (1881) José Antonio Wilde

was intended by those 5 photographs as the accompanying article entitled 'Tango Criollo' made no reference to them and only described men dancing with women. A few months later the magazine included 6 photographs of the same man but on that occasion leading a woman in tango steps. Interestingly the photographs of the two men are frequently seen in books and on social media but the photographs of the man and woman are rarely seen;

- a frequently seen photograph shows men in a dance pose whilst standing in a river. The photograph is frequently referred to as having been taken in 1904 whereas it was taken in 1912. The men were part of a national strike of railway workers who had gathered and passed their time fishing, boating, going for country walks, having asados (barbeques), and engaging in political debates. This is not evidence that it was usual for men to dance tango with men but that men were not averse to pose together in tango positions for a photographer. We can only be grateful that the popular conclusion has not been that 'originally men danced with men in rivers';

Un tango bailado en el agua

- another photograph showed male market traders in a dance hold. Today the photograph is always described as men dancing tango but the accompanying text of the article made no mention of tango nor provided any explanation why the men were posing in that way. It is just an odd photograph.

There are several other photographs (taken in 1907/1908) of social dances where men are dancing with men but clearly it was not because of a shortage of women because not only are there at the same time other men dancing with women but also women dancing with women, and women standing watching. I suggest that men dancing with men and women with women was not considered worthy of comment at the time and it is only in recent years that commentators have created a non-existent back story to justify the behaviour. In North America in 1894/5 the Edison laboratories experimented with moving images and synchronised sound, in what became known as the Dickson Experiment[17]. The film shows a solo violinist playing in to a large receiving horn whilst a couple danced. The two dancers in a close embrace were men. It was not Argentina and it was not tango.

An undated photograph taken in England (estimated to be from the start of the 20th century) shows a public gathering on Blackpool pier, a popular holiday destination. Amongst the crowd are couples dancing in a close embrace – men with women, women with women, and men with men. That was not tango, it was not Argentina, and it was not unusual.

[17] It was arranged and filmed by William Kennedy Laurie Dickson

A different reason given for men dancing with men is not a shortage of women but that they did so to become proficient before inviting a woman on to the floor at a social dance event. This is not a myth but the underlying misunderstanding here is that this was a distinguishing feature of the tango world whereas from at least the 1820s, before the appearance of tango, there were already several dance schools in Buenos Aires that specialised in classes for men only. Men practicing with men belongs no more to the story of tango than to that of the Viennese vals, the polka, mazurka, and the schottische.

8. The Red Rose

If members of the general public were to be asked about the imagery that they associate with tango, then amongst the top answers would surely be the rose in the teeth. It is a perception that can irritate today's tango dancers who explain it away as a ridiculous myth. But there is some basis to the imagery albeit not with a rose and not in the teeth.

From at least the 1820s political factions had identified themselves with coloured flags. In Argentina, the Unitarians (those in favour of a centralised state run from Buenos Aires and culturally allied to Europe) carried blue flags and the Federalists (in favour of empowered provinces and culturally creole) red. The history of

tribal politics in the 19th century was bloody and the new century seemed to be heading in the same direction. In the first decade of the 1900s the Anarchist movement was in full flow with over 50% of adult males in Buenos Aires not politically represented and not entitled to vote (because they were born outside Argentina). 1902 saw the first general strike, there were mass rallies, rent strikes, protests across the country, and in 1905 the Argentine Workers' Federation declared itself to be an anarchist/communist organisation. The panicked government brought in a series of controlling measures including state violence, expulsion of anarchists from the country, laws prohibiting gatherings that spread the socialist/anarchist doctrines and prohibiting the use in any meetings of flags representing proscribed organisations. The colour of the forbidden flag was red. Soon the wearing of a red carnation behind the ear became a defiant accessory of the politically sympathetic compadrito. On 17 October 1908 the magazine *Caras y Caretas* included a full-page colour illustration entitled 'El Tango' of a distinctly working-class couple dancing in a close embrace with the insignia of class politics: the man was wearing a red carnation behind his left ear as a symbol of his political affiliation and the woman was similarly wearing a red flower in her hair[18]. The depiction of working-class men wearing a carnation behind the ear continued: in 1915 the magazine *Fray Mocho* included a drawing, accompanying a piece by Ángel Villoldo, of two immigrants speaking broken Spanish, one of whom had a carnation behind his ear. That floral imagery became horribly distorted when North American film and cartoon makers depicted tango by moving the politically defiant flower from the ear to a flamboyant rose between the teeth. It first appeared in the *The Four Horsemen of the Apocalypse* (1921) a film, starring Rudolph Valentino, based on flamenco that was thereafter confused with tango; in the cartoon *The Gallopin' Gaucho (1928)* Mickey Mouse was seduced by the solo dance to a tango rhythm of Minnie Mouse, rose in teeth; and in the film *Some Like It Hot* (1959) Jack Lemmon and Tony Curtis dance a form of tango each sharing the same rose between their teeth.

---

[18] See cover of this book. The same drawing was included on the cover of the 1910 sheet music for the tango *Don Juan* composed by Ernesto Ponzio.

However for those that knew the history of the class struggle the true meaning of the flower lived on. In the 1940s the orchestra leader Osvaldo Pugliese was arrested several times for his communist political affiliations and his fellow musicians continued to perform in his absence defiantly leaving a single symbolic red carnation lying on the vacant piano.

9. The Illiterate Musicians

The myth is that the early tango musicians and composers were musically illiterate - they could neither read nor write musical notation and were uneducated in musical theory and structure.

By 1880 the number of imported pianos averaged 2500 each year and the importation of piano sheet music grew from 2 tonnes in 1880 to an astonishing 28 tonnes in 1889. The statistics suggest that Argentina did not suffer from a shortage of musicians who could read and play music.

Arturo De Bassi (the composer of tangos that are still regularly heard today) recalled in a 1937 interview[19] how the early pioneering composers of tangos were all assumed to be from the lower social classes as if the association with the upper classes was unimaginable. He heard a description given of himself as a knife-wielding gaucho with wild moustache and military boots whereas Arturo was a rather refined, well-educated, clean-shaven sort of gentleman – a photograph from *Caras y Caretas* on 26 February 1916 captures him perfectly.

[19] after he had retired from the music business

Most tangos, like most pieces of music, were composed and played by those with formal music education. The theatre orchestras, the brass bands, and the rondallas all required the ability to read music scores and to play arranged pieces. So we can dismiss the broad-brush description of musically illiterate tango musicians/composers. But perhaps the myth was intended to more narrowly describe those of the lower-classes who could not afford a privileged education yet still composed and played music. That returns us to the theme of snobbery. We know that some of the pioneers did not receive formal music education and yet composed and played great danceable tangos: Campoamor, Canaro, Greco, Maglio, Esposito. We know that many of the pioneers of the tango we recognise today could read and write musical notation: Bevilacqua, Mendizábel, Posadas, Firpo, De Bassi, Bernstein. We know that a formal musical education did not necessarily lead to good musicianship - many well-educated pianists could not play a decent tango even when presented with the musical score[20]. And so what was the intention of those that peddled the myth - was it derogatory (to infer inferior music) or was it appreciation (of the musicians' success against the odds)? Whatever the reason we need only to recognise the story as untrue and illogical.

Conclusion

There is a saying 'Why spoil a good story with facts?' when good stories are entertaining and easy to tell whilst facts are often neither. But there is a balance to be found and currently the widely held tango beliefs are entirely weighted towards fantasy. So should you, dear reader, encounter friends, family, or general passers-by reciting the many tango myths then please refute, refute, refute until (like me) you become boring.

---

[20] see *Get To Know the Tango Pioneers 1910 to 1919* Part Two/Music sheets

PART THREE

The Fertile Environment

In order to understand the beginnings of tango we must understand the pre-existing conditions from which it gradually evolved. The public was enjoying music and dance long before any identifiable notion of tango emerged and so when it did, often unnoticed, the infrastructure was already in place to allow tango to grow.

There follows two sections highlighting that fertile environment:

1) popular venues where people listened and danced to all kinds of music and where tango made its early appearances: dance halls, cafés, carnivals, circuses, theatres;

2) methods of broadcasting beyond the reach of those venues: recordings, street organs, whistling, sheet music, lyric books, poetry, and films.

Venues

Dance halls, cafés, carnivals, circuses, theatres

1. Dance Halls

In the 1800s Buenos Aires was thriving and no different to any other major city in relation to its choice of all forms of musical entertainment at café-bars, theatres, dance salons, public parks, on the street, and practically everywhere else. It is clear and unsurprising that throughout the developing city of Buenos Aires those that wanted to dance had every opportunity to do so:

- preserved city records reveal that from at least the 1820s there were many approved applications for licensed dance schools and salons. In 1826 we know that the North American William Davis established a dance school in Buenos Aires, formalising instruction in the latest dance styles from Europe and the USA;
- newspapers and magazines published fictional short stories and articles many of which included references to dance, whether as part of the storyline or just as an incidental mention. On 7 January 1899 the entire front page of the magazine *Caras y Caretas* was dedicated to a high society dance event at the home of the wealthy and influential Tornquist family. Inside the same edition was a story about a more informal dance evening described as being in the criollo style. Understandably, just like today, there was very little newspaper coverage of unremarkable, everyday dance gatherings of ordinary folk. However some glimpses did appear and the reader of the Notices section in the magazine *El Ombú* will have seen that in a social club in the barrio of Barracas on

Saturday 12 December 1903 'many couples danced to the sound of a beautiful tango';

- advertisements offered their own glimpses in to the everyday life of dancing:
    - in the 1840s dance halls displayed their prices, generally women could enter free whilst men had to pay and others specified prices per dance;
    - there was no shortage of dance school classes and private tuition;
    - from 1898 bookshops advertised the release of the third edition of the popular Dance Manual;
    - specialist clothing was offered for the dance hall: men's suits, ladies dresses, shoes, and fine white gloves; and
    - in February 1900 an advertisement for a malt extract drink recommended one glass a day to improve one's energy and appearance at the dance halls.

We must not forget that tango music and dance was not limited to the capital city but was widespread through Argentina and the countries of South America. Unsurprisingly, particularly in the summer season[21], the seaside hotels of Mar del Plata regularly advertised their luxurious dance hall schedules and, in the first decade of the 1900s, tangos were a big draw. Further afield in February 1903 *Caras y Caretas* published two photographs taken in the province of Córdoba, northern Argentina. One is of a guitarist with a man and woman 'preparing to dance a tango criollo' and the other entitled 'prelude to a milonga' shows a woman pouring *mate* [22] for a poncho-wearing guitarist. The women are named (Helvecia Ballestrieri and Josefa Schliepa de

[21] December to February in the southern hemisphere

[22] a hot drink similar to tea

Recagno) and both are described as from the 'best of society of Rosario de Santa Fe'. Distinguished society ladies proudly enjoying tangos and milongas. Venturing in to the city of Córdoba itself the construction work on the enlargement of the Grand Hotel Victoria finished in January 1906. Whilst performing there Feliciano Latasa composed a melody based on an old anonymous Spanish song that subsequently became an immensely popular tango. Latasa himself would never know his success as he passed away only a few months later, a week short of his 36th birthday. In Buenos Aires in 1909 his composition *Hotel Victoria* was recorded by the trio (or possibly quartet) of Vicente Greco[23] and in 1910 by the trio Estudiantina Centenario. The tango is best known today by the versions of Francisco Canaro (1935), Juan D'Arienzo (1935, 1948, 1966), Ángel D'Agostino (1945), and Roberto Firpo (1948). The same melody was used later in the tango *La payasa* in the 1924 play *La Borrachera del Tango,* and recorded that same year by singer Ignacio Corsini.

In 1909 a visiting French travel writer and trade emissary, Jules Huret, was invited by the Governor of Salta to a dinner for local dignitaries during which a band played tangos. The dance struck him as 'languorous and lascivious' but not in any way offensive. Huret was not tainted by any preconceptions of, nor any particular interest in, tango - he was a neutral foreign observer whose book of over 500 pages[24] mentioned tango only this once. The dancers were embraced and barely moved, in fact so slowly that he felt he had to explain that 'a good tango dancer takes 30 minutes to make one tour of a room 10 meters long'. He did not

[23] Greco (mis-spelt as Grego on the label) led the first recorded orquesta típica

[24] *De Buenos Aires au Gran Chaco* (1911)

describe the music, other than that the band comprised brass and woodwind instruments but we can make some assumptions from the dance description:

- this was not the fast and energetic tango a*ndaluz* from the theatre;
- it was not some experimental music intended to shock as this was a dinner for the province's ruling class;
- for the same reason the band would have been reputable and formed of trained musicians who could read the music sheets of the different rhythms played;
- the chosen tunes would have been well-known to ensure the enjoyment of the diners and the comfort of the dancers;
- there was no singer (and no lewd lyrics);
- we do not know the chosen tangos but can exclude (thanks to the dance description) the fast tempo compositions like *El porteñito, El choclo, El caburé* and can conjure up something like the 1908 recordings by the Banda Municipal de la Ciudad de Buenos Aires *El irresistible.*

2. Cafés

There was no shortage of café venues in the north, south, east, west and central areas of the city and the playing of tango music was not restricted to any barrio nor for the enjoyment of any particular type of clientele. Additionally hundreds of thousands of residents read accounts in their daily newspapers and magazines about café life and tangos:

- in January 1904 *El País* reported a disturbance in an inner-city refined restaurant that returned to calm once the orchestra resumed its tangos. Contrary to the myths about tango creating disturbances we can draw from this report that not only did tango music have a soothing effect but to have done so by 1904 means it must already have been embedded in the hearts of the citizens;

- on 28 October 1907 the newspaper *La Argentina* said 'there is no café with an orchestra whose repertoire is not dominated by tangos';
- on 5 June 1908 *El Razón* carried a story on a city centre café (on the corner of streets Florida and Tucumán) that the newspaper called 'El Bar de los tangos'. Inside men and women danced in an 'almost aristocratic' setting to the rhythms of fashionable tangos.

It is clear from these contemporary sources that tango music was not confined to the sleazy cafés of the poor barrios and was enjoyed by all throughout the city. For brevity I will focus on just two barrios most commonly linked to the tango story: Palermo in the north and La Boca in the south. It is easy to stereotype these areas (Palermo rich and refined, La Boca the opposite) but that would be misleading. Both areas were populated by the full range of socio-economic residents and visitors and therefore each barrio provided the type of venue and standard of entertainment to best suit the clients.

Palermo

On 11 November 1875 the President of Argentina, Nicolás Avellaneda, opened the first section of transformed parkland in Palermo with the paraphrased words 'The old and rural area of Palermo is from today to be known as El Parque 3 de Febrero that will flaunt its fountains, statues, and avenues amid its artistically laid out gardens that will be illuminated by the arts and all things of good taste to match those parks in New York, Paris, and London'. Already underway was the construction of the zoological garden and the horse racing track both of which are still areas of public attraction today. Immediately thousands of visitors poured in and they all needed food, drink, and entertainment. Makeshift cafés sprung up whilst others submitted planning applications to the Comisión del Parque 3 de Febrero. In 1877 the local dairy owner, by the name of Casares, leased from the Commission a small building for use as a café-bar. Not mentioned in his application (perhaps he did not anticipate it) was the late-night entertainment provided by payadors and the tango pioneers that would draw in the rougher types of the city and the young men from wealthy families looking for excitement. The bar became informally known as El Tambor, Tambito, and Kiosco. In the same year as the opening of El Tambor Juan Hansen applied to the Commission to lease an existing building and convert it in to a restaurant to match the vision of good taste laid out by President Avellaneda. He offered afternoon tea for the day trippers, a restaurant for the evening, and his own attached brewery.

Café Hansen

Officially named Restaurante Parque 3 de Febrero it became known as Café Hansen, or simply Lo de Hansen, and accounts written many years after it was demolished (in 1912) created myths that are still repeated today. The most common is that the

Café Hansen was the 'cradle of tango' which is entirely untrue. There is nothing to link the restaurant with tango during Juan Hansen's tenure, nor during that of his successor Enrique Lamarque in 1893, nor that of his successor. When the 5 year

lease was taken in May 1903 by Anselmo Tarana then tango tales began to be told. I should point out here that although the names of the lease owners changed and the premises were referred to by other names such as El Palermo, Café Tarana (or Lo de Tarana) it was still often referred to as Hansen's - thereby presenting us with some continuity confusion.

On 4 December 1903 the magazine *Caras y Caretas* printed a most glowing report of the new lease holder, Anselmo Tarana, together with two photographs: one of him and the other of an evening scene in the outside patio. In the patio were about 20 men, 3 women and a child sitting at undressed tables with bottles and glasses of beer, and waiters standing by. The article described Señor Anselmo R Tarana as the absolute ideal type of industrious immigrant, a refined gentleman without a stain to his name, running a restaurant that was both luxurious and sophisticated and providing a most delightful orchestra especially brought over from Milan. As part of Tarana's excellent service the customers could be collected from home by one of the restaurant's fleet of cars. This image does not fit well with the descriptions (provided many years later) of rowdy behaviour and coarse tango music. However further investigation reveals a little more about the character of Anselmo Tarana. The newspaper *La Protesta* on 6 May 1906 reported that he was arrested for seriously assaulting a friend at his restaurant. Perhaps his café restaurant was not so

SEÑOR ANSELMO R. TARANA

genteel after all. There is a much-repeated tango story that in 1903 Anselmo Tarana had to take the radical step of pinning up a notice to his customers to say that the playing of Ángel Villoldo's tango *El esquinazo* was strictly prohibited. The problem was allegedly caused by its repeated percussive rhythm that roused customers to accompany the rhythm with their fists and bottles against the tables, and some over-enthusiastic smashing of crockery and chairs for extra emphasis.

An article in *Caras y Caretas,* on 2 June 1928, described the Café Hansen 16 years after the demolition of the building. The author recalled memories from his youth (that I estimate to have been the time of Tarana's ownership) saying that 'In the old days the guys didn't apply hair gel nor drink cocktails but were much tougher'. He remembered how water syphons, glasses, bottles, and tables were regularly thrown and, out in the grounds away from the high society guests, musicians played tangos. Because 'bailongo'[25] was strictly prohibited they surreptitiously danced in the shadows of the garden. An elaboration of his story was made in to the 1937 film *Los Muchachos de Antes No Usaban Gomina*[26] and re-made in 1969. To this day there remains an animated debate (among those that care about this sort of thing) about whether tango was danced at the premises of the former Café Hansen. My contribution is that although dance was not promoted it is safe to assume that when late-night tango music was played to those that usually dance elsewhere, and there were no other regular customers to offend, then of course some would have got up to dance. Often gaps in historical records need to be filled with the question 'what would I have done?'

---

[25] a lower-class informal dance gathering

[26] 'The guys in the old days didn't use hair gel'

The Palermo park

It is worth bearing in mind that the public space of the park itself was a venue for music and dance. On 19 January 1901 the newspaper *El Diario* took the reader on a journey through the park from midnight to dawn when the type of visitor changed. The tone of the article was derogatory. The night-goers were compadritos, often well-known to the police, their heads spinning with alcohol, dressed in the latest street fashions, and accompanied by carriages of girls. The orchestra (a trio of 2 guitars and a violin) started the first notes of a tango 'compadrón' and the dancing was at its peak between 2 and 4 in the morning with couples displaying considerable skills. Almost inevitably as dawn broke the crowd became tired and irascible, one woman refused an invitation to dance a vals, arguments started, punches were thrown and the awaiting police soon intervened. Two men and four women were arrested and the rest of the crowd dispersed leaving as litter an array of clothing, purses, and walking canes. Many citizens reading their morning newspaper were likely to have frowned and associated such uncouth behaviour with tango.

La Boca

Moving to the south of the city in the 1860/70s José and Luisa Tancredi ran a couple of dance halls (known as academies) in the La Boca and San Telmo area. The Tancredis were tough and unhindered by the laws and norms of Buenos Aires society. They crop up in more than a few reported incidents involving unlicensed premises (that was not so unusual), beatings, stabbings, and the use of firearms. In about 1882 the Tancredi dance hall in La Boca was taken over by a local dancer known as Mascarilla who renamed it Bailetín del Palomar. In the absence of further detail we can conjure up an image of the venue. The location and the name is sufficiently evocative. It was in the dockside barrio of La Boca and named Bailetín (indicating a modest dance space) and Palomar (being a pigeon coop). The well-regarded tango dancer Mascarilla was Juan Filiberto, father of the soon to be tango pioneer Juan De Dios Filiberto.

Today's tourist visiting Buenos Aires will undoubtedly, but probably only once, walk the pedestrianised street known as Caminito in the barrio of La Boca. The area is an outdoors tango museum providing visitors with souvenirs, performing street dancers, and glimpses of life in the early 20th century conventillos. But it is six blocks beyond the protected area of Caminito that lies the crossroads where many of the pioneering tango greats performed every night. To reach the area today it is necessary to ignore the advice of the policemen (whose job it is to discourage tourists from roaming in to one of the deprived and potentially dangerous areas of Buenos Aires) and head north for two blocks to the street of Suarez then turn east towards the Río de la Plata until you come to the junction with Necochea. The walk is neither attractive nor recommended and when you arrive today you are faced with dilapidated two storey buildings coloured with graffiti, streets littered with discarded cardboard, and a growing sense of unease. In 1908 Necochea was the main street along which businesses prospered day and night. The area was thriving as the centre of transatlantic and South American sea trade and there was a vibrant flow of goods, people, and services at a time of continued mass migration from Europe and from the Argentinian provinces and city outskirts. Even today the dockside bridge and cranes dominate the skyline at the end of Necochea. There is nothing there today to interest the tango visitor and so let us stand at the crossroads and imagine we are in 1908 accompanying an eager tango fan who does not want to miss out on any of the night's performances. Standing at the crossroads and walking a few doors down on Necochea on the left-hand side heading towards the docks is number 1221 a magnificent, stone fronted and balcony-bedecked building:

- the Café Royal was more affectionately known as Café del Griego after the ostentatious Greek owner Nicolás

Bardaka, a man with jet black curly hair, a handlebar moustache, and a gold medallion hanging from his coloured jacket. Moving around the tables were waitresses, dressed in the European style of black with white aprons, and raised high above them almost at ceiling height was a small mezzanine space like a theatre box with a piano bolted to the wall. Up there were three musicians playing tango. The main attraction was the bandoneón player with his instrument that was becoming the defining sound of the new version of tango. The bandoneonist was Vicente Loduca, the pianist Samuel Castriota, and the violinist Francisco Canaro.

From the Café Royal the (imaginary) tango fan crosses the narrow road to the Café Eden opposite:

- commonly known as Café de la Turca after its female proprietor of Turkish origin. The exterior of the building was not as grand as the Royal but inside was just as busy. A trio was playing tango: the brothers Vicente and Domingo Greco on bandoneón and guitar respectively with Ricardo Gaudenzio on violin.

In order to sample more tango delights in the area it was necessary to leave Café Eden, cross the street again and go in to the premises next to the Café Royal:

- this was the Café Concert, at number 1224, and inside was a solo performer: the 47-year-old Ángel Villoldo. He was a recording star and represented the earlier world of tango before the bandoneón craze.

Although there were more cafés to choose from in Necochea our imaginary tango fan returned to the corner and turned right in to the street of Suarez heading for number 275, a much more modest, single-story building in the Spanish adobe style:

- at the time of writing the building remains today as it was then. In 1908 it was called La Marina and inside was bandoneonist Arturo Bernstein, a regular and favourite of La Boca cafés. On other evenings at La Marina one could catch the bandoneonist Genaro Espósito, known as 'El Tano' (the Italian) with violinist Agustín Bardi and guitarist Félix Camarano.

We cannot know the repertoire of those musicians but Francisco Canaro, in his autobiography, remembered the tangos most frequently played during those years as including: Manuel Campoamor's *La cara de la luna, El Sargento Cabral, En el séptimo cielo,* and *Ahí nomas*; Alfredo Bevilacqua's *Apolo, Venus,* and *Recuerdos de la pampa;* Ángel Villoldo's *El choclo, El porteñito,* and *El torito*; Vicente Greco's *El pibe* and *El morochito*; Roberto Firpo's *El compinche*; Arturo De Bassi's *La catrera*; Ernesto Ponzio's *Don Juan*; Enrique Saborido's *La morocha* and *Felicia*; Prudencio Aragón's *El talar* and *El Pardo Cejas;* Carlos Posada's *El toto* and *La llorona;* Lorenzo Logatti's *El irresistible;* and others without assigned composers such as *Siete palabras* and *El llorón.* Some of these are still heard today thanks to the later (preserved and available) recordings of orchestras in the 1930s to 1950s whereas other, no lesser, tangos have sadly not reached the ears of 21st century tango fans.

Today's visitor to Buenos Aires can sample the café environment of some of the venues that were open during the years of this book (but not necessarily hosting tango music) particularly those that are advertised on the official list of Bares Notables. Sadly there seem to be closures each year but at time of writing those still open include La Biela (established 1850) in Recoleta, Café Tortoni (1858) in Centro, El Federal (1864) in San Telmo, Los 36 Billares (1894) in Centro, Café Margot (1904) in Boedo, and La Flor (1907) in Barracas.

3. Carnivals

The Carnival is an annual festival in the Christian calendar celebrated in February/March (40 days before Easter) and involves public parades, music, dance, and the wearing of disguises. The tradition precedes the Christian adaptation. In ancient Rome celebrations involved the inversion of the social order assisted by the wearing of masks and disguises so that slaves could sit at the head of the table whilst their masters served them. Across the Americas it was the Africans that dominated the carnivals as they were by far the largest under-class and so were allowed to enjoy a day or two pretending that the social order had been reversed. In 1822 the newspaper *El Argos* report noted that 'the most distinguished people stoop to behaviour that must be called barbarous . . . showing every sign of having lost their reason; and sometimes we see them associating with the grossest sort of plebeians'.

The music and dance parades in the annual February and March carnivals were dominated by black societies or 'nations'. The Buenos Aires *Gazeta Mercantil* of June 1842 counted about 30 black nations (such as Moros, Angola, Cabunda, Banguela, Conga, Rubulo) largely based in and around the 'barrios de *tambor*' in San Telmo and Montserrat next to the river and port. However their dominance of the carnival was challenged and changed over the coming decades by the arrivals in to the city of European immigrants and countryside creoles. Dating from as early as 1810 there are reports about the attendance of white Europeans at the black dance halls and in 1835 a French traveller wrote that a dance of Africans was accompanied by the strumming of a guitar by a 'gringo compadrito'. The carnival article in the Buenos Aires newspaper *El Nacional* on 5 January 1863 included descriptions of the black revellers dressed as kings, singing and dancing their candombes and playing their drums whilst ignoring the disruptive, alcohol-drinking whites. Gradually the non-black partying population muscled in to the processions. Some commentators say that this was done mockingly but I feel it was more likely to have been an adaption than a mockery just as white musicians during later years 'culturally appropriated' blues, jazz, rock and roll, soul, and rap. In 1870 a French visitor had noted that the parades were full of whites with painted black faces, wearing similar clothing and playing similar music to the black Argentinian 'nations'. Despite being an outsider he could discern the differences in quality: 'they are entertaining themselves but no others and are certainly not allowed in to any of the salons'.

In an article in *Caras y Caretas* on 15 February 1902 the journalist interviewed two elderly black ladies who described how, from about 1870, the long-established African traditions at carnivals were being copied and inevitably changed (in their view for the worse) to such an extent that the black population started to withdraw their participation. The wife of the last 'King' of the Venguela Nation[27] described how in the past (namely pre-1870s) the women were at the head of the parade dancing candombe followed by the marching musicians. She named her uncle Tomás from Montserrat who carried and played the large drum whilst her cousin Joaquín the much smaller marimba drum. The appreciative crowds applauded, threw flowers and sometimes money but all of that changed when the gringos joined the parade with their faces blackened, imitating the accents and cries of the black

[27] the 'Nations' were societies to retain aspects of the African culture and the 'King' was the symbolic head.

participants, and crudely adapting the candombe body movements to the gringo rhythms. She said that there was not a single gringo in the city who had not at some time blackened his face to pretend that he was part of the Venguela Nation[28]. We should remember that for the black population this annual public expression had deep cultural and religious roots and the invasion and trivialisation, which they saw as mockery, was for them a humiliation. The Venguela Nation, like many others, withdrew from the carnivals leaving the annual event to develop in to bizarre fancy-dress parades peppered with the throwing of water bombs and eggs.

By the start of the 1890s the dominance of the black carnival had completely changed. In 1890 an advertisement in the Montevideo newspaper *La Razón* promoted a luxury carnival dance event at the New Politeama theatre with space to comfortably hold 2,000 dancing couples but the entry was explicitly 'not permitted for people of colour'. Although it was still permissible to pretend to be people of colour. In Buenos Aires in 1891 the Sociedad de los Negros Congos posed for a photograph in their parade uniforms, flags, candombe drums, guitar and assorted instruments and although their faces were blackened their facial features clearly show that they were not from the Congo. In 1892 in Buenos Aires one of the white carnival societies, Los Artesanos de Barracas, chose a local boy to be their mascot and walk at the head of the procession. The 8-year-old Agustín Bardi found himself in the middle of the carnival entertainment that included the music of candombe drums, habaneras, tango andaluz, mazurkas, and polkas. For him that day proved to be a formative event. He grew to become an influential composer whose tangos still regularly fill today's dance floors around the world through the recordings of orchestra leaders Francisco Canaro, Juan D'Arienzo, Carlos Di

[28] in 1870 the carnival society La Africana (being whites with painted black faces) is known to have played one habanera and one tango

Sarli, Lucio Demare, Edgardo Donato, Osvaldo Pugliese, Ricardo Tanturi, Aníbal Troilo and others from 1932 to 1954[29].

The annual carnivals were not only street parades but also involved ticketed events in the mainstream venues such as Teatro Politeama, Teatro Nacional Norte, and El Pabellón de las Rosas, thereby attracting revellers from across the socio-economic spectrum. In 1895 the Teatro Victoria was adapted to host the carnival that during the February season attracted 2600 revellers. The newspapers enticingly reported that the best tangos were

played there although frustratingly they did not name their titles. On 18 February 1899 *Caras y Caretas* helpfully included a cartoon showing the participants of that year's carnival parade depicted as a payador on foot carrying a guitar, a gaucho on horseback also with guitar, a black candombe drummer, and a horse-drawn carriage with white revellers in various disguises. The accompanying text further described a group of creoles dancing the traditional gato, prado, huella, pericón, llanto, and malambo whilst singing the 'melancholy songs of the Pampas that were poetic and carrying the untamed spirit of the open lands'. Here we can see the mix of popular dance genres in to which would fit very easily the developing 'tango argentino'. On 8 February 1902 *El Pais* reported that over 100,000 happy people had passed

[29] See *Get To Know the Tango Pioneers 1910 to 1919*

through the streets to the modern rhythms of the voluptuous habanera and the creole tango.

In 1903 the dominant music and dance at the carnival changed. A dance newcomer was described in the newspapers as being performed well by the blacks but spoilt when attempted by the white population. The dance had already conquered the elegant ballrooms of Paris having come from North America. It was the cake-walk. Carnival articles declared the death of tango (in 1903) and the rise of what one described as 'a tango from Africa' and another said that the cake-walk 'is our tango translated in to English by the yankees'. Another article had an accompanying drawing of a couple dancing the cake-walk with a high society man in long tail tuxedo and bow tie incongruously in the company of candombe drums, 'the tangos were danced in the style of the cake-walk'. However, tango fought back and two carnivals later in March 1905 *Caras y Caretas* declared 'At the carnival the tango has made itself the owner and master of all the dance programmes'. Every theatre was announcing new tangos and the Teatro Victoria in particular was 'full of happy people in disguises: the tough guys from the edge of town, the boys from the nice families, and the girls who are even nicer. As soon as the orchestra starts playing tango the partners get together, embrace, and dance as if putting all their desires in to it'. Tango was further described as the working-class dance 'par excellence'. But it was not only for the working class. On 24 February 1906 the Teatro Casino (where *El Pais* noted 'there, like all the dance halls, the tango ruled from start to finish') held its first masked ball and gave various prizes to those revellers that they considered to be wearing the best disguises, to the couple who danced the best tango with cortes, and the couple who danced the best vals without cortes. Their selection of prizes included four 18 carat gold bracelets (one with diamonds and sapphires, one with a single ruby and two sapphires, one with just diamonds, and the other only plain gold); an 18 carat gold chain with pearls; a couple of 18 carat gold rings adorned with a sapphire and a ruby, and lower down the prize list was merely a watch on a chain. It is not difficult to guess the social class of the participating tango dancers. In *El Pais* that year the observing journalist was not impressed by the upper-class attendees pretending to be compadritos with ridiculous exaggerated dance moves. It was in some ways reminiscent of the carnivals 30 years earlier when the white population tried to adopt the music and movements of the black dancers.

In the closing years of the decade the mass gatherings from across the social spectrum of Buenos Aires were dancing to their favourite music, tango:

- In February 1907 the main theatres of the Nacional, Argentino, Opera, Casino, San Martín, Victoria, Marconi, and the Buckingham Palace were all full of dancers and it was the tango that was 'banishing' all the other forms of music;
- in February 1909 the Teatro Victoria music programme was 'tangos, tangos, y tangos'.

1905 Teatro Victoria during carnival

4. Circuses

The tango historian's attention is drawn to the circus from the 1850s not because of the familiar acts of gymnastics and trained animal shows but because of the introduction of musical entertainment in the intervals. It was not evident at the time but we can now see those musical interludes as significant developments in the growth of a home-grown creole culture in to which tango naturally fitted. The appetite was for national artists performing national songs. In the years 1855 to 1858 the newspapers frequently reported on circuses that interspersed the acts with short plays of heroic gauchos enlivened by singing and dancing with orchestras playing 'agreeable music'. The performances attracted large audiences from a wide cross-section of society. In 1887 the newspaper *El Diario* reported that the Podestá Circus production was so successful that the police were called in to control the queues. In November 1890 the newspaper *Súd America* expressed its surprise that even the Buenos Aires social élite had turned their attention away from Italian operas towards creole plays and many decades later the circus empresario José Podestá recalled that the former national president Domingo Faustino Sarmiento was once amongst his circus audience.

We can get an impression of the circus era by watching the film *La Cabalgata del Circo*[30] that, although released in 1945, does faithfully recreate the history of the creole circus genre as it developed in to the theatre and finally in to the world of film. *La Cabalgata del Circo* declares itself a 'Homage to the artists of the heroic circus who beneath the canvas tent gave life to the freedom and justice of the creole pantomimes. To all of them: the Podestás, Scotti, Rafetto, Carló, Cassano, Anselmi etc creators of a breed of artists we dedicate this procession'. The film shows realistically

[30] the musical director of the film was Mario Maurano, director of the Orquesta Típica Victor (1943-44)

enough the journey of the country song to the city and the changing styles of tango. We can see inside the circus tent a small orchestra playing and a couple singing in the Spanish zarzuela style; later a gaucho enters the tent on horseback, playing guitar and serenading his love in the precursor style of the tango canción; followed by a fast tango andaluz version of the tango *El caburé* to the supposed sounds of an organito; and briefly a rendition of the tango *El porteñito.*

5. Theatres

In the second half of the 19th century in Buenos Aires the architectural revolution, based on the Parisian model, included the construction of grand theatres. Today we are familiar with the internal design of a standard theatre: a raised stage at one end, rows upon rows of fixed seating in the centre, and on both side walls extra seating often in compartmentalised boxes. That image makes it difficult to imagine how the Buenos Aires theatres were also home to the circus and to carnival dances. The above photograph of the San Martin theatre in 1890 shows that the auditorium chairs were not fixed and so the space could be used for, in this case, a circus ring or completely cleared to accommodate a vast dance hall. In the previous *Carnival* section the photograph of the Teatro Victoria (p60) shows spectators in the boxed seating whilst the main auditorium floor is used for dancing. The theatres were also used to present stage performances in the familiar manner. A particularly popular form of production was the zarzuela, a theatrical play of Spanish origin largely conducted in song and dance.

In 1890 there were 700 zarzuela productions in Buenos Aires, the following year there were over 1000, by 1895 nearly 4000 and by 1897 they completely dominated at 75% of all forms of stage entertainment in the city. As a large part of the city's population at that time was Italian some theatres specialised in presenting their productions in the Italian language. In 1895 when a million people went to see Buenos Aires zarzuelas 120,000 of them attended the Italian language versions. Their popularity was not shared by everyone. An 1893 report by the Buenos Aires city council stated that these 'new zarzuelas are corrupting the city's artistic theatre'.

Cultural tensions

Whilst many in the theatre audiences were recent European immigrants the majority were by then second and later generations who expected a more relevant national content, particularly as they had become accustomed to the creole circus reflecting the Argentinian culture. In 1857 a Spanish zarzuela company put on *The Gaucho of Buenos Aires* in which the Spanish actor, musician, singer, and composer Sebastián Ramos performed two tangos one of which was *Tomá mate, che*[31]. More Spanish zarzuela companies tried to adjust their content by replacing their regular song of the Spanish jota with milongas and habaneras, their flamenco-style foot stomping with tangos, and their Iberian accents to criollo. Their efforts were not totally convincing and so they recruited local actors and singers for the parts of gauchos and porteños - thereby increasing creole influence in the content and delivery. In one zarzuela the character of the housekeeper had a song and dance routine to a (now anonymously composed) tune that was a typical tango andaluz. The music was printed and sold (as *Señora Casera* and *Tango de la Casera* in 1880) and became popular throughout the city. When words were added they varied according to the context and the singer but somebody (now unknown) added local Buenos Aires lyrics and renamed it *Andate a la Recoleta* (Get yourself to Recoleta). In more recent times it has become known as the first tango criollo but it is not safe to make such a claim. The music was composed for the light-hearted Spanish-style theatre. Simply adding some local references to the lyrics did not make it a distinctly Argentinian tango.

Furthermore there was a certain audience unease about being entertained by the former colonial masters when Argentina was trying to establish its own identity. The nationalist tension was also felt the other way around for example on 25 May 1895 a Spanish theatrical troupe refused to stand and sing the Argentinian national anthem causing an uproar in the Teatro Rivadavia. In the same year a Spanish actress purported to sing the national anthem but replaced the words to insult Argentina resulting in a predictable riot and her earlier than expected departure back to the Iberian Peninsula. Similar political tensions continued across the country and reinforced the need for a national theatre genre.

---

[31] a version of which was later recorded by Alfredo Gobbi in about 1907 and much later by Francisco Canaro with singer Alberto Arenas in 1951.

The brothers of the Podestá circus family (Pablo, Pepe, Gerónimo, and Antonio) took advantage of these changes in public taste by expanding their circus interval plays in to a full theatre production for one season. That experiment established them as the founders of the 'teatro rioplatense', the genre that broke away from Spanish and European dominance to reflect the culture of the area of the Río de la Plata bringing to the fore local actors, accents, local themes, music and dance. This in turn led to the emergence of tango, albeit still in a different form to that known by 21st century tango fans. It seems to me that this home-grown culture was deliberately accelerated and celebrated and, to a certain extent, deliberately enjoyed almost as a point of national pride more than as in response to its inherent artistic value.

On 28 September 1897 the zarzuela *Justicia Criolla* put tango argentino on centre stage in the theatre land of Buenos Aires. The musical director was Antonio Reynoso (left) whose tango compositions were recorded by various artists between 1902 and 1908. In one scene set in the central patio of a conventillo an actor proposed that they started with a tango and (the musicians) could strum the strings of their guitars and as the others began to dance another cried out:

I am the tango. Look at me. This is how it is danced.

The message was clear: 'This is this city's tango, not Spain's and not Cuba's, and this is how we dance our tango'.

On 27 January 1898 at the Teatro Apolo the Podestá family opened their play *Ensalada Criolla*, the setting of which was also in

a conventillo and in one scene three couples danced tangos. The title, meaning a mixed salad, referred to a mix of tangos, milongas, habaneras, and the main characters of a black man, a mixed-race gaucho type, and a blonde woman. Buenos Aires was celebrating itself as an 'ensalada criolla'.

On 17 July 1902 in the play *Fumadas* the character played by Pablo Podestá (above) was taught how to dance tango with cortes. Whether the characters were heroes or figures of fun the introduction of themes linked to the poorer classes and to tango had started to infiltrate the minds and the interests of the city's theatre-going population whose preferences changed. Statistics from 1904 show that 275,000 people went to see Spanish-style zarzuelas whereas an ever-increasing 400,000 went to see the home-grown creole productions.

Carlos M. Pacheco

Although the precise beginning of any artistic genre is difficult to pinpoint to a particular date, studies of the Argentinian theatre identify 1906 as the year that the creole theatre truly established itself as a popular genre with the production of two plays by Carlos Mauricio Pacheco. His speciality was the tragicomedy based entirely on the local themes of creoles, immigrants, compadritos, anarchists, thieves, milongueras[32], and tango all mixed together in the setting of the conventillos of the poorer barrios. In 1906 his play *Musica Criolla* included a rendition of the tango *La morocha* using the words of Ángel Villoldo plus a sentimental tango. In the closing scenes of *Musica Criolla* two characters discussed the wonder and contrasts within tango music by saying:
Isn't tango both sad and happy at the same time? There it is, that's music criolla!
Today's aficionados of tango music will recognise that same dichotomy of feelings.

The newspaper *La Argentina*, on 28 October 1907, captured the general mood of theatre land when it described the scene of

[32] women from the poorer barrios making a life for themselves in the world of show-business

crowds pouring out of the theatres, whistling and singing tangos. Theatres, their plays, and their music reached everybody regardless of their socio-economic status or their pre-conceived prejudices.

Another emerging playwright was José González Castillo (below) who from 1905 to 1909 put on *Los rebeldes, Del fango,* and *El retrato del pibe* the latter of which opened with the whistling of a tango. Over the coming decades he and his son would become a prolific tango duo of composer and lyricist[33].

[33] See the books *Get To Know the Tango Pioneers 1910 to 1919* and *1920 to 1935.*

Broadcasting

Recordings, street organs, whistling,
sheet music, lyric books, poetry, films, publications

1. Recordings

The Beginnings

The 1850s saw the beginnings of a technological revolution - the ability to 'etch' the sound of the human voice - but it was not until the 1880s that its commercial application began to take hold in the world of musical entertainment. Fortuitously that timing coincided perfectly with the rise of tango and so, without having the slightest knowledge of the emerging culture of the Río de la Plata, the inventors of recorded sound are now amongst the key pioneers that created the fertile environment in which tango was able to flourish. After other brilliant minds in Europe had developed the concepts of capturing speech and developed crude proto-types it was Thomas Edison (right) who unintentionally discovered the most successful method. Edison's original focus was the telegraph. He was developing the means to send multiple messages on an apparatus involving a rotating disc with a pivoted arm embossing on paper the dot and dash signals received from the telegraph line. When speeded up Edison noticed that the embossed points created a single tone like a musical note. Intrigued by the effect he wrote in his notebook on 18 July 1877 that he was speaking in to a diaphragm that indented in to rotating paraffin paper and the vibrations made slight indentations that could then be replayed. By August he had

developed a rotating cylinder covered with tin foil and tested it in front of his workers at his laboratory in New Jersey. Not knowing that his first demonstrated words were to become historically significant he decided to recite a well-known verse, the nursery rhyme 'Mary had a little lamb, its fleece was white as snow, and everywhere that Mary went the lamb was sure to go', much to the amusement and puzzlement of his staff. Now connected to the second diaphragm he turned the cylinder and out came his words. The phonograph was the only voice in the room as everyone else was stunned in to silence. After securing his patent on 15 January 1878 he turned his mind to its practical application which at that moment was still completely unclear. In the *North American Journal* of 1878 he listed the potential Top Ten uses: the first was to replace stenographers with one's own dictation[34], further down the list at number four was the envisaged recording of music narrowly ahead of the benefits of recording the last words of a dying relative. His phonograph invention was exhibited extensively in the Americas, including in Argentina, but its complexities were too much for the general public's non-expert use and within a year even Edison tired of it as he busied himself with the imagined possibilities of creating light with electricity.

The flat disc

Various adaptations to the cylinder were made by others but the game changer to recorded sound came with the intervention of Emile Berliner. Having made his own improvements to the cylinder phonograph and named his version the Gramophone in 1887 he soon changed from the cylinder to a disc. He made it with zinc, coated with wax, and the stylus etched a line moving from side to side rather than Edison's preferred movement of up and

[34] that particular idea failed immediately due to the resistance of the surprised labour union of stenographers

down. Emile needed a machinist to produce his gramophones and he found one in the back streets of Camden, New Jersey, in a workshop tucked away at the rear of a horse carriage company. The owner, Eldridge Johnson, was not impressed with the design and described the sound as like a partially educated parrot with a sore throat and a cold in the head. The two of them nevertheless developed a professional understanding and before not too long (1900) a small business was formed, called the Consolidated Talking Machine Company, that (after a challenge and a victory in court) was renamed the Victor Talking Machine Company. Over the coming years the advantages to the buying public of the disc format became clear:

- by increasing the disc diameter size, reducing the spacing of the grooves, and (from 1904) introducing double-sided discs meant that the playback time increased from the cylinder's 2 minutes up to 5 minutes per side[35];
- it was easier and cheaper to reproduce multiple copies from a master disc than a master cylinder;
- the disc had a centre for an informative label rather than only on the external packaging;
- and being flat a collection of discs was more convenient to store at home.

From a technical point of view there were some aural challenges from both cylinder and disc recordings that may not have been apparent to most listeners:

- a background hum that came from reverberation within the receiving horn;
- the diaphragm could only capture a limited frequency range of somewhere between 160 to 2000 hertz whereas the human ear detects from 20 to 20,000 hertz. That meant the musicians had to adapt to play in the middle ranges, avoiding the full scale of their instruments,

[35] Although cylinders limped on until 1930

thereby not reflecting their more expressive live performances;

- the vibrations of stringed instruments (including double bass and piano) created a muffled, muddy sound. That meant that more 'phonogenic' instruments were preferred - like the crisp metallic sound of brass. That resulted in a disproportionately higher number of brass band recordings that can mislead us to believe that they were the most popular form of live entertainment when they were not;
- the balance of instruments was variable in that the nearest or loudest could dominate the others, as there was no post-recording mixing option;
- there was only a limited amount of recording time that could be captured and so long classical pieces came in an extensive collection of 2 or 3 minute individual recordings. Once this aspect had occurred to me, I realised that often tango recordings from the 1900s seem to just fizzle out without an emphasised ending, especially absent is the now familiar 'chan chan' ending. It is almost as if they played until they received the engineer's signal to bring it to a stop.

Despite all of the challenges the quality of the recordings delivered to the customer was excellent. There are several accounts from that time, including from impressed professional opera singers, that likened the recordings to having the singer/musician in the same room. In 1905 an advertisement for the gramophone 'La Victoria' showed its popularity: in the home of a relaxing couple; at an upper-class dance event with men dressed in formal tuxedo attire; outside at a family gathering in the park; and on stage at a full theatre accompanying the star female singer. Yet when we listen to cylinders and discs from that decade the degraded sound is far too distorted to comprehend how anybody could have enjoyed the experience. We should remember that we are not listening to the same sound. The buying customers knew that the recordings had limited life span and would soon wear out due to the needle eroding the finely precise contours of the groove and they would buy replacement discs as necessary. In 1905 Pathé boasted about its new long-lasting sapphire needle and pointed out that other needles on the market had to be changed after just one play. It is easy to imagine that many customers were not so diligent with their replacement of needles and the erosion of the groove was severe. Today we are listening to more than a century's worth of often inappropriate needles having carved their way around the fragile recordings. Audio historians are in many ways similar to archaeologists that still marvel at broken fragments although they know that they will never experience the fully formed beauty of the original article.

The multi-national talking machine companies

Between the 1890s and 1909 the acceleration and proliferation of commercial activity around the new technology of sound recording was astounding. The fuller story of the formation of the recording companies, their ownership, their patents, their markets, and their labels is complicated and vitriolic. Alliances were formed, contracts broken, trading names proliferated, machine patents infringed, composers' works improperly copied, artists' names misrepresented, and legal injunctions were plentiful [36] . Even within the same parent companies the subsidiaries were subject to buy-outs, mergers, and cartel agreements resulting in a frequently changing regime of ownership, control, and market share. In the USA and in Europe the leading names (that were not entirely independent of each other) included the companies of Gramophone and Typewriter, Universal Talking Machine, International Talking Machine, Victor Talking Machine, Columbia Phonograph, Zonophone, Odeon, Parlophon, Edison, and Pathé. Additionally there were many smaller companies that were either absorbed in to the amorphous web of aggressive international players or simply disappeared after a few years of operation. Particularly in Europe there were many smaller and successful recording companies that after 1910 were acquired by the corporate empire of Carl Lindström AG. In the face of dynamic competition the international companies raced to expand their markets around the world variously coming to agreements to carve out regions between them. The main drive was to sell their machines and their own cylinders/discs but also to expand the market further by sending engineers with specially adapted mobile recording machines to capture local music in different countries[37]. Before we peer at the history of recordings too intently through the tango lens I need to be clear that there was nothing perceived to be particularly attractive about music coming out of Buenos Aires. The visits to Argentina were part of a global expedition and at the same time other engineers were heading for Africa, the Indian sub-continent, the Middle East, the Far East, and everywhere else. Establishing global commercial dominance was the driver rather

[36] see *Gold Rush* below

[37] the Victor Talking Machine Company was slightly behind others as it only developed its own portable recording equipment in late 1902

than any esoteric desire to safeguard and share ethnic musical heritage. The end result however was the successful preservation of musical history for future generations.

Tangos recorded outside Argentina

Before we turn to the recording of local artists in Buenos Aires it is worth noting that a substantial number of tangos had already been recorded in both Europe and North America that were neither composed nor performed by artists from Argentina. There were fast tangos from Spain, often adorned by castanets; slower tangos with a distinct Cuban habanera rhythm; and easy listening tangos from multi-genre orchestras. From as early as March 1894 to the end of 1909 at least 50 different recordings were made of *La Paloma*[38], both instrumental and with singers all in a variety of different styles. In 1900 Cuban soprano Rosalia Chalia recorded *Tango del Café*; in 1901 North American Carlos Francisco recorded several tangos including *Tango de los Negritos*; in 1902 Antonio Vargas, a Mexican baritone opera singer, recorded the Andalucian tangos *El morrongo*, *El lapicero*, *El Negrito y La Mulata*, *El relámpago*, and *Tango toros de puntas*. In the latter the habanera rhythm can be heard amidst the castanets.

Gradually from 1905 there appeared a few tangos that had been composed (but still not performed) by Argentinians:

- in England on 2 May 1905 the Royal Military Band recorded *Guido* and *la Payada* both composed by José Roncallo;
- in the USA in July 1906 the Orquesta Argentina Victor (a brass band of North American session musicians) spent a few days in the Victor laboratory[39] recording 14 tangos including those composed by: Alfredo Bevilacqua (*Apolo*), José Roncallo (*Ché, sacámele el molde)*, Rosendo

[38] variously described as tango, habanera, or other genres

[39] the recording rooms were not called studios for many years to come

Mendizábal (*Club Z* and *Reina de Saba)*, Enrique Saborido (*La morocha)* and Ángel Villoldo (*El porteñito* and *El choclo*);

- in France in 1907 the brass band of the Paris Republican Guard made a series of recordings that included Manuel Campoamor's tango *El Sargento Cabral*;
- in France in 1908 the Band of the Paris Republican Guard recorded nearly 60 tangos included Juan Bergamino's composition *Joaquina* (today we are familiar with the versions by Juan D'Arienzo 1935, 1943, 1953), and others composed by Ángel Villoldo;
- in 1909/1910 the North American Orquesta Victor recorded tangos by Villoldo and other Buenos Aires composers.

Recordings in Argentina

On 24 February 1878 the *Courrier de la Plata* reported that the city's telephone and telegraph company, Cayol y Newman, had been granted licence to manufacture the Edison cylinder phonograph. On 29 December that year *El Mosquito* advertised the exhibition of the 'phonograph known as the talking machine' during which voices, spoken and sung, were recorded and played back to much excitement. Cayol[40] y Newman continued to make phonographs for the relatively few technology enthusiasts who recorded family, friends, and professional performers. It is not possible to say which artists were recorded as the cylinders have long since disintegrated but we do know that in 1893 the Podestá Circus was touring the northern province of Tucumán with its production of *Juan Moreira* when it treated its audience to a live audio recording. They brought out to the circus ring a cylinder phonograph and sang in to the recording horn and then played it back to the amazement of all. That particular cylinder of course no longer exists but was

[40] Carlos Cayol's son was Roberto Lino Cayol (born 1883) who became a prolific tango lyricist and playwright

undoubtedly amongst the first professionally performed creole songs recorded in Argentina.

In early 1900 the tango *El automóvil* was recorded on cylinder at the Buenos Aires Teatro Mayo. The song was from the Spanish zarzuela *El Ultimo Chulo* (first performed in Madrid in November 1899) and performed by the leading actor José Palmada. An indication of that tango's popularity was the story on the front page of the Spanish newspaper *La Correspondencia Miltar* on 9 April 1900. Two altar boys, who were supposed to have been guarding the remains of a saint in a Seville chapel, had been seen practicing the dance of the tango *El automóvil*. We should pause for a moment and think back to the entrenched myth of the earliest tangos being danced in Buenos Aires brothels and re-imagine it re-told as being first danced by choristers in the crypts of Andalucian chapels. The latter seems ridiculous yet neither tale deserves to be elevated to the defining image of tango.

Buenos Aires

Buenos Aires retailers started to import and specialise in talking machines with the accompanying cylinders and discs. They became the promoters of local artists, with several providing the city's first recording laboratories in partnership with the international record companies.

- From January 1899 the department store Guppy on the Calle Florida (photograph above) began to advertise its range of cylinder phonographs for both sale and hire[41]. In August it published an explanation of the talking machine accompanied by a drawing showing two family members listening via earphones made of rubber tubes, similar to a doctor's stethoscope. This was remarkable technology. It

further explained that the Edison phonograph could record voice, song, and music and re-record up to 10 times on the same cylinder. In October it advertised a more substantially built phonograph with the ability to record voices. Here we can see the battery power pack, the storage tray of

[41] Guppy specialised in talking machines, bicycles, and small firearms.

cylinders, the cylinder and of course the horn that both receives and emits sound[42].

- In November and December 1900 the retailer Piccardo Palmada (trading as The New Century) offered its 'phonograph laboratory with electricity in perfect working order' in which the customer could 'record cylinders, whether speaking or singing and in which there is a splendid piano and other instruments'.

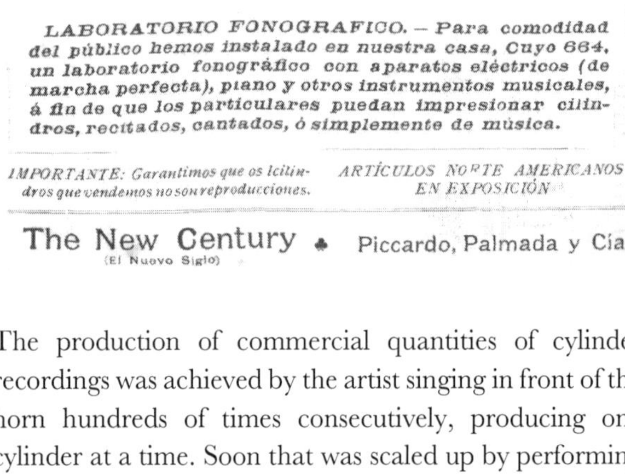

LABORATORIO FONOGRAFICO. — Para comodidad del público hemos instalado en nuestra casa, Cuyo 664, un laboratorio fonográfico con aparatos eléctricos (de marcha perfecta), piano y otros instrumentos musicales, á fin de que los particulares puedan impresionar cilindros, recitados, cantados, ó simplemente de música.

IMPORTANTE: Garantimos que os lcilindros que vendemos no son reproducciones.

ARTÍCULOS NORTE AMERICANOS EN EXPOSICIÓN

The New Century (El Nuevo Siglo) ♣ Piccardo, Palmada y Cía

The production of commercial quantities of cylinder recordings was achieved by the artist singing in front of the horn hundreds of times consecutively, producing one cylinder at a time. Soon that was scaled up by performing in to multiple horns each directed to its own cylinder. Further multiplication was attempted by playing the cylinders themselves in to recording machines (without the artist present) but inevitably that created much lower quality recordings.

[42] in 1902 Guppy was taken over by the retailer Laborde who recorded their own cylinder selection of payadors and local brass bands

• The retailers Cassels and M. E. Repetto could not have been more different to each other but are to be forever linked because they were pioneering adversaries. Cassels was a large prestigious department store on the Calle Florida selling multiple household items. M.E Repetto was a ship's chandlers, paint and iron goods store a long way from the fashionable shopping areas. In February 1900 the Gramophone Company advertised their auditorium in the premises of

Cassels and, in July, Cassels themselves published a photograph of their gramophone department in which customers could listen to a selection of North American and European machines and discs prior to purchasing. On the left of the room you can see a framed painting of the soon to be globally recognised image of a dog being attentive to 'his master's voice'.

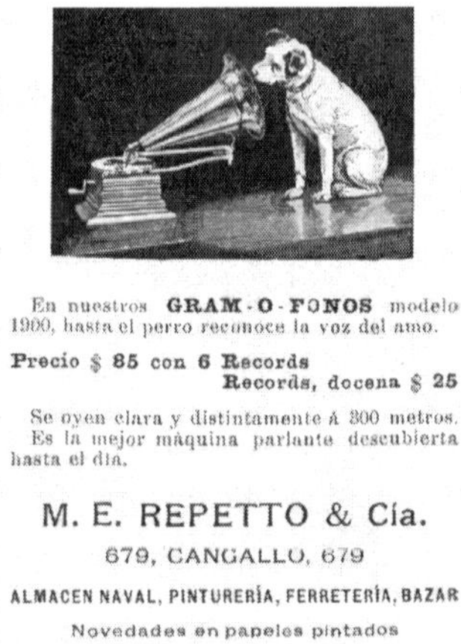

On 19 May 1900 M. E. Repetto advertised gramophones and discs (also using the still unbranded image of a dog staring in to the acoustic horn). Said to be the best of its type the sound could be heard clearly up to 300 metres away [43] . By January 1901 Repetto had imported recorded discs manufactured in Milan, Madrid, Paris, Vienna, London, and New York and boasted that because it was not a formal agent for any of the record companies it could offer discs at much cheaper prices. Cassels turned to the Supreme Court of Justice and secured an order preventing Repetto from trading in gramophones and discs [44] . Undeterred by the on-going legal action, in March 1901 Repetto got over-excited and teased its customers: 'coming soon will be discs with creole songs'. Over a year later, on 23 August 1902, Repetto advertised its creole discs (below). They were the first disc recordings in Buenos Aires and included the singers Arturo Navas and Alfredo Munilla, the Banda de Policía de Buenos Aires (led by José Rizutti), and the Orquesta de Teatro San Martin. The best-selling, at 100 discs a day, was *La carcajada del Negro Juan* sung by Arturo Navas (and composed by his payador father Juan de Nava).

[43] there is separate evidence of machines being used to entertain crowds at outside fairs and other events

[44] on appeal that was overturned in July 1901

Amongst the many recordings were a few tangos:

- *Ensalada criolla* from the play by Eduardo García Lalanne;
- *Los pilletes* from the play by Nemesio Trejo and Antonio Reynoso;
- *Dejá é jugar, ché!* and *Bartolo tenía una flauta* sung by Alfredo Munilla and composed by Ángel Villoldo.

Cassels were not impressed by the sound of Repetto's recordings and warned the public not to be cheated by others who supplied poorer quality goods with 'acutely discordant sound'. They needed to recover the market lead and on 19 March 1904 made an important (but over-optimistic) announcement: 'due to arrive shortly in this city a special team from Gramophone with the most modern of equipment to record bands, songs, recitations, and other national pieces'. They were positioning themselves as the sole approved agent of the major recording companies and the sole provider of locally recorded discs. Unfortunately Gramophone let them down as the company did not have the resources to spare. In September 1905 the trade magazine *Talking Machine World* revealed the alternative arrangements: Cassels were sending Argentinian artists to both New York and Paris to record 'native Argentine songs and music. This has been found necessary in order to meet the demands of their business'. Cassels sent two artists, Diego Munilla and Eugenio Gerardo López, to the recording laboratories of the Gramophone and Typewriter Company in London and Paris. López was a popular reciter of poems, prose, and political debates whilst Munilla was a singer/guitarist of creole airs. Amongst Munilla's recordings was *Bartolo toca la flauta*, a traditional song delivered in the style of a milonga/tango. Two years later Cassels finally secured their visiting team of experts. On 7 September 1907 Bill Nafey[45] embarked on a sea journey to Buenos Aires and became the first recording engineer of the Victor Talking Machine Company to visit South America. He recorded about 130 tracks that included several tangos that are familiar to us today: *El incendio* by the Banda Italo-Argentina; *Hotel Victoria* and *El porteñito* by the Banda de la Policia de Buenos Aires; *El irresistible, El choclo* and *Cosa linda barata* by the Banda Municipal de la Ciudad de Buenos Aires; and *Z Club* by the Orquesta del Teatro Apolo.

[45] Nafey was responsible for designing and building the first recording facility for Eldridge Johnson (founder of Victor Talking Machines) in 1898 and remained central to Victor's recording history

- The Casa Lepage on the Calle Bolivar and Avenida de Mayo was principally a photographic retailer. The owner, Belgian immigrant

Don Enrique Lepage, tundador de la «Casa Lepage».

Señor Max Glücksmann, continuador de la obra de Lepage.

Henri Lepage[46], had already expanded in to the new technology of moving images when he further extended his interests in to the market of recorded sound. On 1 January 1899 Lepage advertised the ability to bring the theatre in to the home with recordings of the human voice and music. Initially the advertisements promoted recordings of imported opera and classical music but within a few months the Lepage catalogue included well-known tangos from the theatre. I suspect that Lepage made their own recordings on Edison phonographs (manufactured in Buenos Aires by Cayol y Newman). Lepage retired and returned to Belgium and in August 1908 the Casa Lepage announced that the new owner was Max Glücksmann[47]. On 25 September 1909 Glücksmann advertised double-sided Victor discs under the 'New Creole Repertoire' series that included recordings of 'famous bands, orchestras, singers, and real

---

[46] named Enrique in Argentina

[47] during the following decades Max Glücksmann became one of the most influential promoters in Argentina of tango recordings, tango radio, and tango film. See *Get To Know the Tango Pioneers 1910 to 1919* and *1920 to 1935*

payadors'. They included tangos (still familiar today) such as *Yunta brava, El choclo, No le hagas caso, Si te perdes chiflame, El incendio,* and *Reina de Saba* recorded in Buenos Aires by the Banda Municipal and the Banda Italo-Argentina. There were also country songs by Alfredo Gobbi, Arturo Navas, and Domingo Munilla[48]; comic songs by Ángel Villoldo and Alfredo Gobbi; and a range of other rhythms by the Banda de Policía de Buenos Aires, the Banda Militar, and the Orquesta del Teatro Apolo de Buenos Aires. Notably they were all advertised as playing in the generic style of an 'aire criollo' – tangos were just another form of national music, a creole air.

- The Casa Tagini on the corner of Calle Perú and the Avenida de Mayo was owned by the brothers José (Giuseppe) and Juan Bautista Tagini, and specialised in the new technology of talking machines[49]. From May 1903 they advertised their imported phonograph, graphophones, and gramophones with discs and cylinders from Edison, Victor, and the Gramophone Company and, in 1904, became the exclusive

[48] Diego and Domingo Munilla were sometimes referred to at the time as the Munilla Brothers. Whether they were related is still debated today.

[49] José and Juan operated separate arms of the Tagini business

distributors for the Columbia Phonograph Company. By March 1905 they claimed to have more than 30,000 cylinders and discs for customers to choose from and that its gramophones had substituted for live musicians at over 1000 dance events. In 1907 Tagini were retailing

Odeon discs recorded in Buenos Aires that included tangos by Ángel Villoldo (*El porteñito, La bicicleta*), by the Banda de Buenos Aires (*No le hagas caso*), by Linda Thelma (*La morocha*), by Manuel Campoamor, the Rondalla Vázquez and several more. On 20 November 1909 two engineers (William Freiberg and Gus Forbush) from the Columbia Phonograph Company arrived in Buenos Aires and headed for the Casa Tagini to make recordings. Amongst their many tango recordings were those by the 'orquesta típica criolla especial' of Vicente Greco – an immensely significant event in the history of Argentine tango music. Greco's tangos included *Rosendo* and *Don Juan*. These were the first recordings of a group that included the bandoneón and the style of tango was significantly different to those of singer/guitarists, the brass bands, and theatre orchestras. The North American magazine *Music Trade Review* (in March and

April 1910) reported that Columbia had received a large batch of masters recorded at Buenos Aires that the manager of the Export Department described as 'the finest and very best records made in that part of the world' for which they already had large orders. The discs were shipped back to Buenos Aires in May 1910 and they were first advertised on 30 July 1910 by Casa Tagini. That was the start of the promotion and popularity of the new tango groups known as orquestas típicas[50].

- The retailer Fonografía Pathé, on the central Avenida de Mayo, had for several years been selling records of European artists, mainly French and Italian operatic and theatre singers. However on 15 August 1908 it advertised its records of the stars of the Buenos Aires creole theatre including Pablo Podestá, Los Gobbi, sisters Aida and Olinda Bozán, and 50 tangos criollos 'recorded especially for dances'.

- The Casa Edison in Buenos Aires was one of only six regional headquarters outside of New York, the others being in London, Berlin, Paris, Sydney, and Mexico City. Its advertisements, whilst always reminding its readers about the inferior products sold by other retailers, pushed its cylinders on which its customers could record their own voice and instruments, something that could not be done on discs. Edison, unlike the other retailers, did not record professional artists in Buenos Aires. In November 1907 Walter Stevens, the head of the recording section

[50] see *Get To Know the Tango Pioneers 1910 to 1919* and *1920 to 1935*

of the National Phonograph Company (effectively Edison since 1896), told *Talking Machine World* 'we could have sent a team of engineers down there (to Buenos Aires) but we are too busy and cannot spare a single man[51]'. He did concede that it did not make economic sense to send artists from Argentina to New York. Despite that concern *Talking Machine World* reported again in June 1909 that 'several artists from Buenos Ayres are in New York, recording songs and popular music of the Argentines. The instrumental records are also arranged by this native talent for the same market.'

Before leaving this section on the pioneering retailers I ought to mention the grand department store of Gath & Chaves, due to its prominent place in the frequently told story of early tango. The store supposedly sponsored the singers Alfredo and Flora Gobbi, Ángel Villoldo and others to go to Paris to record on the Gath & Chaves label. That claim has elevated the retailer to be seen as one of the main pioneering promoters of tango recordings but it is an undeserved position[52]. In all of their weekly advertising in newspapers & magazines from 1905 onwards the undoubtedly magnificent store sold every imaginable product for the home (imported from Paris, London, and New York) and yet they never positioned themselves as sellers of gramophones and discs nor did they ever promote local creole musicians. There were recordings (including tangos) produced on the Gath & Chaves label but I suspect that they were recorded by Pathé and simply branded with the reputable name of Gath & Chaves for the Buenos Aires market. Pathé separately did occasionally advertise that Gath & Chaves was their only approved retailer in Buenos Aires.

---

[51] at that time Edison was manufacturing 100,000 cylinders a day

[52] the Gobbis recorded prolifically in Europe but barely on a Gath & Chaves label and there is no evidence that Villoldo went to Europe.

Summary

Prior to 1910 most of the cylinder and disc recordings made in Buenos Aires were not tangos. However, the context of Buenos Aires tango in the opening decade of the 1900s is provided by a joint advertisement on 1 January 1906 by Cassels and Lepage (and the Montevideo agent Dellazoppa). Included in a footnote in tiny text, barely intended to be noticed, is a description of the offered recordings as 'faithfully reflecting the beautiful characteristics of national aires: tangos, vidalitas, tristes, bailes etc'. Tango was amongst the mainstream Argentinian musical genres but it was not always identified as a separate genre (it was certainly not separated as something shocking or shameful). It was just another beautiful national 'air'.

The Recording Industry's 'Gold Rush'

The recording industry in the first decade of the 1900s was a form of gold rush. It developed faster than its good governance, regulation, and laws. It was a world of cut-throat competition, opportunism, chicanery, and in some cases fraud.

The retailer Cassels was determined to prevent local competition and pursued a civil action against the retailer M.E.Repetto. The image of Nipper the dog staring in to the horn of a gramophone was established as a trademark by the USA Patent Office on 10 July 1900 and thereafter used by Eldridge Johnson of the newly formed Victor Talking Machine Company. Cassels had used a copy of the original painting prior to the USA patent, which anyway did not have any legal standing in Argentina. Cassels challenged Repetto's right to use the image in its advertisements and specifically the image printed on Victor discs imported by

Repetto. One such consignment was impounded at the port awaiting a judicial decision. Although Repetto was trading lawfully with Victor, whose discs labels bore their USA patented trademark, it was Cassels that had the exclusive right as an Argentine national company to use that trademark in Argentina. As a result the discs were released to Repetto but with all of the labels destroyed. This led to Repetto registering the trademark of Royal Records in Argentina and re-labelling the discs accordingly[53].

In September 1907 the Buenos Aires Casa Edison advertised its phonographs and cylinders as 'genuine and legitimate', an opening warning to other retailers who may be selling improperly imported or counterfeit products. The following month the Edison advertisement became more specific 'We judge it necessary to warn the public that we are the only branch in Argentina for the sale of Edison phonographs, cylinders and other products. The sale by anybody else is forbidden. If you are unsure about the legitimacy of a retailer then please ask us'. Edison was relentless in its pursuit of unapproved retailers. In June 1908 its advertisement in *Caras y Caretas* declared in bold print 'We do not have a branch in Rosario' and requested its customers who had been cheated by this unscrupulous retailer to get in touch.

The Casa Tagini was also fighting unlawful competition. Despite having secured exclusive distribution licences (to sell discs labelled Marconi, Fonotipia, and Odeon) others in Buenos Aires were sourcing them and/or creating counterfeit copies. On 15 September 1908 at the Buenos Aires Civil Courts the Judge Rodriguez Larreta ruled in favour of Casa Tagini's contractual rights to be the sole agent in Argentina to receive and sell records of the label Fonotopia and Odeon. In doing so he ruled

53 discs also bore the label of Zonophone, by then a subsidiary of Victor

that other businesses selling, or purporting to sell, those records were doing so illegally and 8000 records were seized as a result. That was a great victory for Tagini and for the public who up to that point had been buying pirated or counterfeit records unknowingly.

Allegations, claims, and counter-claims would continue over the next decade regarding the sale of illegal copies and discs falsely purporting to be of famous artists.

6. The 'DJs'

The appearance of gramophones in venues of public entertainment created a new role: the person who changed the records. On 11 March 1905 (during the carnival period) a Casa Tagini advertisement included a drawing of a man attending to his gramophone and playing dance records in what appears to be a converted space in a stable – the horse is just visible to the left

(above). Gramophones were also in cafés and shops simply to provide background music. A 1905 photograph shows a Buenos

Aires shoe polish and repair shop at the rear of which is a woman

operating a gramophone to play recorded music for the customers inside and for those within earshot outside as they went about their normal daily business. We should remind ourselves that (despite the tango myths) the male customers did not immediately resort to dancing with one another, nor break in to knife fights, nor start cavorting with prostitutes. Tango music was normal and enjoyable but not of course for everybody. In March 1907 in *Caras y Caretas* another photograph appeared of a shoe polish business with customers, staff, and a prominent gramophone but the journalist was clearly not enamoured by the relentless blast of recorded tango music - 'the horror of the tango made a deep impression upon me and caused much shame. I wanted to run away'.

From September 1906 Victor Talking Machines began to market a gramophone produced as a piece of elegant furniture rather than a technical machine. The gramophone, including its horn, was housed within a range of wooden cabinets suitable for all homes from apartments to mansions and was branded as the

Victrola. That brand name soon became synonymous for all gramophones and the person putting on the discs, often a woman,

was known as a *victrolera*. You can see a victrolera portrayed in the 1949 film *Pantalones Cortos* that is based on Buenos Aires life in the early 1900s.

7. Street organs

The portable organ, known as an organito, was a street or barrel organ that came in all shapes and sizes ranging from the lightweight version with straps around the operators' shoulders to those on horse-drawn trailers to entertain crowds at fiestas in the parks. The organito has become an embedded image of the pioneering days of Buenos Aires tango and is commemorated in the titles and lyrics of many tangos that are danced at today's milongas [54] . However, its sound was

8 June 1901

[54] for example *Organito de la Tarde, Organito Callejero, Organito del suburbio*

already a familiar one long before the emergence of tango. In 1853 the author of Argentinian gaucho literature, Hilario Ascasubi, referred to the street organito. In 1859 the *Manual de la Isla de Cuba* described how the portable organitos were played in the streets by day and night and that the music was in two parts, each one with repeated phrasing of eight beats of two by four[55]; 'at first both the music and the dance are calm as if the soul and body are finding their way but then it gets spicy, sometimes sad sometimes happy, but always passionate as the couples flow flirtatiously and charmingly as much with their hearts as with their feet'. This wonderful description could equally apply to today's tango social dances anywhere in the world. In 1888 Buenos Aires the journalist Casimiro Prieto wrote about the street organitos producing the dance music for gatherings of the lower classes. In 1898 José Maria Ramos Mejía, the city's director of health and education, assessed the impact of the high volume of new immigrants on Buenos Aires: 'although many were industrious and dressed well they still behaved crudely in social setting…and they preferred the street music of the organito to the classics'. The organito was not just a city phenomenon as, back in 1872, the Argentinian epic poem *El Gaucho Martin Fierro,* set in the countryside, described how a young girl was dancing to a tune wound out of an organito operated by a gringo. In 1883 Ventura Lynch, the researcher of Argentinian folk music and dance, wrote that the organitos had introduced to the gauchos the international vals, habanera, polka, and mazurka.

At the end of the 19th century we start to see mention of tangos associated with organitos:

- On 3 December 1898 *Caras y Caretas* published a short story entitled 'Street Scenes of the Organito' with drawings of a large organito on a two wheeled handcart. On a Saturday evening the two operators, Italian

[55] a similar construction to the tangos yet to emerge

immigrants Giacomo and Pietro, pulled it from their conventillo through the streets calling out 'It's the organ, let's dance!' and soon small crowds gathered to do just that. They paid the operators to play tanguitos (a Spanish tango andaluz), habaneras, valses, and mazurkas and danced in the street until they were moved on by the local policeman. Giacomo and Pietro continued all night attracting small groups with their mobile orchestra until at dawn they returned home to their conventillo. This would have been a familiar scene for the readers in 1898.

- On 22 March 1902 *Caras y Caretas* published a drawing and article depicting a petition by street organito operators complaining to the Mayor of Buenos Aires about his new law compelling payment of royalties per song. They warned that if they went out of business then the conventillos would die as their organitos were the only things that brightened the lives of the residents who loved to dance to the polkas, tangos, milongas, and fandangos. Of course the organito did not brighten everybody's lives. A few months later a cartoon entitled *Buenos Aires Lírico* made fun of the citizens of the city being plagued by music wherever they went, such as organitos in the street when trying to sleep or work.

- In 1903 the magazine *El Gladiador* included a short story about a conventillo in Buenos Aires where a young lady from Madrid was dancing a typical zarzuela when an Italian immigrant who had wheeled in his organ on a cart started to play tangos. It was him that attracted the residents and soon a couple danced in the middle of the patio, both agile in close embrace and to the cheers of the crowd they performed their first corte with quebrada. The Spanish zarzuela was beaten by a tango argentino. Conjuring up a similar scene in October 1904 *Caras y Caretas* published a poem entitled 'El Tango' accompanied by a drawing of a couple dancing in a close embrace. The poem described a lower-class scene where the silence was broken by the sound of tango from an organito and a young man and woman (after exchanging coarse words) began to dance with her skirt brushing the dust of the yard in 'voluptuous quebradas'.

8. Whistling

Despite all of the technological wonders of the late 1800s we should not forget that one of the most effective broadcasting media during this period was the human whistle. Whistling popular tunes in the street was a catchy method of spreading personal recommendations. Early popular tangos (that are still known today) such *as El incendio, La chiflada, La cachafaz, El apache argentino* all start with a distinct call most suitable to the human whistle. On 28 October 1907 the newspaper *La Argentina* had noticed that because every family home and café was playing fashionable tangos the streets were now full of people whistling tangos.

But it was not only people that whistled tangos. There are some accounts of tram drivers using their warning horns to emulate the opening whistling melodies of popular tangos, undoubtedly to the amusement of those nearby who were tango fans and to the irritation of those who were not. On 17 April 1898 the magazine *Buenos Aires* named the tram driver 'Juan José' as the best player of the warning horn crossing the city blasting out popular melodies that included tangos and milongas. We will never know which particular tunes were broadcast in this way but we can be satisfied that they were not the tunes of an obscure sub-culture but were so popular that they were instantly recognisable by a few introductory notes.

9. Sheet Music

In February 1901 the Buenos Aires newspaper *El Tiempo* included an advertisement for the sheet music of 14 tangos by the Breyer Brothers music shop (that had been selling pianos since 1882[56]). In 1905 another company, Tonini, offered music for the stringed zither ('that any child could play') listing over 100 pieces of every type of musical genre including 'tango criollo'. Tango was beginning to blend into mainstream popular music to such an extent that across the city adults and children were playing it on a variety of instruments in their homes.

Printed music sheets of 'tangos for piano' were becoming popular and included not only compositions from the theatre but also 'tangos criollos' for dancing. The sheet music provides us with historical documents of the popular tangos but I must add a note of caution that although they contain the recognisable melody

[56] at time of writing is still doing so in central Buenos Aires

they are not an accurate transcription of exactly how the music was played by the artist at the time. The musical notation of the tangos was most often done by a third party - that is, neither the composer nor by a tango musician - so that the resulting product was a simplified version that was intended to be played by any mediocre home pianist. In 1910 the musician and tango fan Osman Perez Freire became so frustrated by his peers' spiritless piano renditions that, in order to help replicate the correct rhythm and 'edge' of the true tango, he designed his own tango notation[57].

Printed sheet music was not only for the private use of amateurs but was essential for professional musicians in orchestras, brass bands, and rondallas who performed in front of large audiences spreading the sound of tango. The sheet music was also exported to other countries thereby spreading the music to much wider audiences: the Royal Military Band (England 1905) and the Orchestra Argentina Victor (USA 1906) recorded tangos composed in Argentina with sheet music printed in Buenos Aires.

10. Lyric Books

There had long been a public appetite to read the words of all popular songs and the appearance of tango lyrics was another route of broadcasting the genre. On sale from at least the mid-1800s in Argentina were the full scripts of theatre plays (zarzuelas) including the words of the songs, several of which were tangos. Similarly newspapers and magazines printed, sometimes taking a whole page, the words of particularly successful stage songs (again often tangos). There is a myth that the lyrics of tangos were obscene and were part of the reason for tango's rejection by decent society. There are some examples of tango titles and lyrics with sexual innuendo but they were consistent with the style of other genres (in Argentina and around the world) and were

[57] published in his monthly magazine *Álbum Musical Centenario*

thoroughly enjoyed by the wide cross-section of society that heard them in the theatres and read the words in books and newspapers[58].

Specialist compilation song books were published under the series *Biblioteca Gauchesca* and *Biblioteca Criolla* and included the lyrics of popular Argentinian folk songs such as cifras, vidalitas, estilos, and milongas. In 1903 the payador Manuel Cientofante (right) created his own magazine *El Ombú* the first edition of which included the words of his tango *La Gaucha* 'in her hips the tango, in her eyes the estilo' – a reference to the continuous mix of creole styles (tango and estilo). 1907 saw the release of a new collection of his previously unpublished verses that included many cifras, decimas, estilos, mazurkas, vals, habaneras and two tangos:

- *Los Cincuenta* (that is similar in content to Ángel Villodo's *Cuidado con los cincuenta)* a reference to the recent law that fined men 50 pesos for publicly 'complimenting' women; and
- *La Cangela* that included the line 'the tango has already begun boys, let's dance but don't forget the 50 for a compliment'.

In October 1908 *Caras y Caretas* included a full-page article entitled 'El Tango' including ten verses of lyrics referencing female sensuality and the macho male, the mixture of the soul of the Pampas milonga, the Spanish gypsy and the gringo together with music from the accordion, violin, and piano. The article made no

[58] the tangos for the dance halls were always instrumentals (no lyrics, no singers)

criticism of the music, the dance, nor the lyrics - this was simply a celebration of tango from the poorer barrios[59].

In 1909 the Buenos Aires magazine *En La Vereda* (On the Street) published the lyrics of a number of tangos including the ever-present *El porteñito*. In the same year a songbook entitled *Tangos Populares* included the lyrics of *El choclo, Los 50*[60], *El morocho* (being *La morocha* adapted for male singers), a vals, and a milonga together with a cover drawing of a couple dancing tango.

11. Poetry

The words of tangos up to the first decade of the 1900s were not considered to be poetry any more than are today's pop songs. The lyrics were intended to make people laugh - they were happy, cheeky, and sometimes controversial. On the other hand folk songs had lyrics to be listened to - they were thought-provoking (whether sentimentally or politically) and were considered to be poetry from the early 1800s. Most poets, of course, produced their verses without any association with music. One such poet was Evaristo Carriego (right) who was born in 1883 and died in 1912 and is today perceived as a pioneering tango poet. He was not but he did inspire later tango poets. In 1908 he published a book of poems *Misas herejes* (Heretical Masses) romanticising the Buenos Aires slums

[59] often described as 'tango arrabal', the arrabal being the fringes of the city

[60] this is *Cuidado con los 50,* a tango still heard today but as an instrumental

and the lives of the residents. In 150 pages of verses he mentioned the word 'tango' only twice:

- 'al compas de un tango, que es *La morocha*' (to the beat of a tango, that is *La Morocha*);
- 'esta noche en el Casino cuando te entusiasme el tango' (tonight at the Casino when you get excited by the tango).

His verses also included references to musicians, the organito, guitar, flute, and clarinet, and other dances: the sad cielito, the pericon, and habanera. His real influence on tango was that many of his poetic themes[61] were continued in the lyrics of tangos by later playwrights and particularly, in the 1940s, by poets such as Homero Manzi and Homero Expósito whose lyrics are now enjoyed by today's tango fans. However his personal connection to tango was tenuous as illustrated by his obituary. Immediately following news of his death the magazine *Sherlock Holmes* published a full-page eulogy to him admiring his simple yet honest verses demonstrating the affection in which he was held by the artistic world. There was no mention of tango nor of lyrics for any form of music. Despite that he has nevertheless found himself to have been immortalised within tango history, mainly due to:

- the 1930 book entitled *Evaristo Carriego* by Jorge Luis Borges [62] who mixed up a supposed biography of Carriego together with a broad description of life in Buenos Aires that also included tango; and
- the instrumental tango, *A Evaristo Carriego,* recorded by Osvaldo Pugliese in 1969.

12. Films

In July 1883 the Buenos Aires newspaper *El Nacional* described a show at the Politeama Theatre in which projected moving images were shown - the forerunners of the coming film industry. It was

---

[61] nostalgia, lost loves, and the lives of the 'noble' working classes

[62] Carriego was a close friend of Borge's father

achieved by still photographs on a rotating disc projected on to a screen. The images included a couple dancing, what appears to be a vals, in a close embrace (although the woman's left arm was hanging free rather than holding the man).

Three years later *El Nacional* reported 'Cinematografo' moving images at the Teatro Odeon that delighted the public with well-known scenes of the near countryside. Moving images were generating increased public interest and Argentinian pioneers were bringing them relevant short films. Possibly as early as 1906 Eugenio Py made a short film called *Tango Argentino* or *Tango Criollo* (it is now lost and so the estimated date and the description relies on memories gathered by film historians). It is believed to have been shown in Europe and the USA as part of Argentina's cultural outreach to expand trade and investment and is said to have featured Buenos Aires dancers. The least we can say is that the making, and international promotion, of such a film in 1906 is another piece of evidence to counter the myth that tango was regarded as shameful and shunned by the Argentinian establishment.

Prior to 1910 Eugenio Py experimented with sound by recording actors and singers on to a cylinder whilst filming them. The film was then projected at the same time as the recorded voice[63]. These short films, now lost, are said to have included Ángel Villoldo and the husband and wife team Alfredo and Flora Gobbi performing popular theatre songs from the plays *Ensalada Criolla*, *Justicia Criolla* and others written by Antonio Reynoso, Nemesio Trejo, Eduardo García Lalanne, Antonio Podestá and other pioneers of the creole genre. We can only hope that someday these short films will be found and shared.

---

[63] in 1909 the British Vivaphone sound-synchronisation system had successfully matched film and sound recordings

13. Publications

It is evident from the multiple references in this book that tango music, lyrics, and dance were mentioned frequently in the many newspapers and magazines on sale in Argentina during the late 1800s/early 1900s. The articles obviously provide us with historical information but they also demonstrate that by placing tango under the noses of a broad section of the population those newspapers and magazines were themselves influential broadcasters of tango culture.

PART FOUR

The Pioneers

Dancers, singers, brass bands, rondallas, pianists, bandoneonists, violinists, flautists, guitarists

1. Dancers

Many successful promoters of the Argentinian tango dance were Europeans in Europe:

- in November and December 1905 at the Palais Royal in Paris Aimée Campton (English) and Marthe Derminy (French) danced tango together. Aimée as the lead dressed in male clothing (right). Tango was already creating a great commotion in Paris and they became two highly celebrated proponents;
- in 1906 the already famous Italian opera singer Olympia D'Avigny paired up with the Buenos Aires dancer María Cores (who played the male lead) to dance tango. So successful were they (largely due to Olympia's existing reputation) that they went on to tour Paris, Madrid, Lisbon and other European cities;
- in 1907 the Frenchman Tod Cams organised the first European tango dance competitions (first held in Nice and then Paris). He changed his name in 1908 to the more aristocratic-sounding Camille De Rhynal and by 1913/14 had gone global organising the first World Tango Championships;
- in 1909 there was a hit show entitled *Le Criollo* at the Folies Bergères, Paris in which two actresses (one dressed as a man) danced 'tango argentin', the music of which was published to great success.

In Argentina itself there were of course many dancers of tango but only a few are known, largely from anecdotal memoirs and interviews. The dancers came from the theatre and the circus, from the humble dance halls through to the exclusive ballrooms, and from the street. I will risk some over-simplification by putting them in to categories.

1) Stage performers. Many actors and actresses danced tango on stage and subsequently have been described as tango dancers. Most of them were not committed dancers of social tango and certainly did not become pivotal in the pioneering development of the tango dance form, but some did.

- Elías Alippi was born in 1883 and in 1904 he danced a tango on stage in the play *Justicia Criolla* and off-stage was a regular and well-regarded dancer at the fashionable dance venues. His plays and films (as both an actor and producer) often included tango music and dance scenes and a couple of years before he died he appeared as the tango dancer Alberto in the 1939 film *Asi es la vida*[64].

- Arturo Navas (de Navas or Nava) was born in 1876 in Uruguay and became a successful singer/guitarist, like his payador father Juan. In the 1890s he performed in the circus and the theatre and by 1902 was taking the leading roles as singer, actor and tango dancer. On 7 February 1903 in *Caras y Caretas* Arturo appeared in five photographs in an article entitled 'Tango Criollo' that bemoaned the end of traditional tango. Arturo was shown in various tango holds with another man, both dressed in country attire, and the

A. DE NAVA

[64] the film's musical director was tango pianist and composer Enrique Delfino

background was a roughly built single storey building suggesting that they were in the countryside or on the fringes of the city. Six months later, on 5 August 1903, Arturo appeared again in photographs in another article entitled 'Tango Criollo'. Again he was dressed in country clothes and again in various tango holds but that time with a woman partner.

2) Working class men

- Juan Filiberto, known as 'La Mascarilla', was a man of many trades from being a weightlifter in the Rafetto Circus, a sailor on the boats from La Boca, and a tango dancer whose reputation attracted other dancers (and musicians) to his dance hall Bailetín el Palomar. In 1885 he also became the father of Juan De Dios Filiberto tango musician and composer from the 1920s to the 1950s;

- Casimiro Ain, born in Buenos Aires in 1882, was excited by the visiting street organito to which he and his friends danced freestyle. When a little older Casimiro joined the circus troupe of Frank Brown, multi-tasking as required, but principally as a dancer during the musical intervals. In a later interview he recalled that at the age of 19, in 1901, he worked his passage on a merchant ship that took him to England and from there he made his way to Paris. By 1903 he was earning a few francs dancing what he later described as tango criollo accompanied by two friends on an old guitar and violin. There are no further details of his dance style nor the music. Casimiro returned to Buenos Aires and married Marta who became his dance partner and in 1904 they danced tango on stage at the theatres of the Opera, Politeama, and Casino. In 1913 Casimiro travelled to Paris and to the

USA with a tango trio of musicians from Buenos Aires who made their own historic impact[65];

- Alfredo, known as 'El Rey de los Negros' danced tango in the barrio of Flores. He was also well connected to the wider tango scene: his father-in-law is said to have been the composer and pianist Rosendo Mendizábal and his half-brother the bandoneonist and tango composer Jorge Machado;

- Pedrín known as 'El Tuerto' (one-eyed) in the barrio of San Telmo specialised in energetic tangos with sharp cuts (cortes), apparently whistling his own tango melodies as he danced;

- another Pedrín known as 'La Vieja' was born in 1881, also in San Telmo, and was a neighbour and friend of Domingo Greco (the older brother of bandoneonist Vicente). In adolescence, before 1900, Pedrín was known as an outstanding tango dancer - combining speed with refinement, creativity with musicality. The better known 'El Cachafez' was described as a mere imitator of the great Pedrín;

- Benito Bianquet (later known as 'El Cachafaz') was born in 1885 and made his name dancing tango on the streets around the market of Abasto. In the early 1900s he ventured in to the area of Palermo and challenged the skills of local tango dancing hero, the black Argentinian 'El Pardo' Santillán, thereby securing the spread of his fame. Bianquet re-lived his early dance style in the films *Tango* (1933) and *Carnavales de Antaño* (1940[66]) although by

---

[65] See *Get To Know the Tango Pioneers 1910 to 1919*

[66] storyline set in the about 1912

then he had already long ago adapted to a more refined style in order to teach and entertain the wealthier set in both Buenos Aires and Paris.

3) Upper class men:

- Daniel Videla Dorna and Ricardo Güiraldes (both of whom we have met on page 20) travelled to Paris in 1901/1902 where they demonstrated the dance and taught it to the high society.

- Alberto López Buchardo also travelled to Paris, in about 1906, where he danced, played piano, composed, organised tango events, and later brought over dancers and musicians from Buenos Aires;

- Vicente Madero, born in 1884, was the party-loving son of a wealthy family and in the opening decade of the 1900s developed an elegant tango style based entirely on the walk with long gliding steps, rather than the contemporary style of energetic cortes and quebradas;

- 'El Flaco' Saul, a son of Argentinian landowners, mastered both the styles of rapid complicated figures and the smoother, calmer glide depending on the venue and the abilities of his partner.

4) Women from the dance halls:

- The dancer Concepción Amaya ran the tango venue known as Lo de Mamita. Singer songwriter Ángel Villoldo played there, as did violinist Ernesto Ponzio and flautist Luis Teisseire. The passed down tale is that Concepción ran off with tango pianist Sergio

Mendizábal (the brother of the better-known Rosendo);

- Joaquina Marán was a regular dancer at Lo de Mamita and later organised her own events. The guitarist and singer Juan Bergamino dedicated to her a tango that he named *La China Joaquina*. We know it today by the shortened title *Joaquina* later recorded by Juan D'Arienzo (1935, 1943, 1953) and Francisco Canaro (1939, 1955);

- Laurentina Monserrat ran the dance venue Lo de Laura and for the dancers she is said to have hired the tango pioneers: pianist Rosendo Mendizábal, violinist Ernesto Ponzio, and bandoneonist Vicente Greco.

2. Singers

It is often said that the early tangos were not sung which is confusing because there were many singers of tangos in the 1890s to 1909. What is meant is that tango dance music was instrumental and other tangos were sung.

Accepting that there are always exceptions I have ventured four categories of singers that influenced the sung tango:

- those from the popular theatre. The lyrics were part of the play's storyline, most often humorous, and delivered by actors rather than by professional singers. The words were more important than the voice. This genre of tango song is reflected in the compositions and recording style of Ángel Villoldo and Alfredo Gobbi;

- those from the payador and singer/songwriter world. The lyrics were observational (whether sentimental or political) and demanded attention. The words were more important than the voice. This genre of tango song is reflected in the composition and recording style of Gabino Ezeiza, Higinio Cazón, and Pancho Cuevas;

- those specialising in songs knowns as *tonaladas* and *cuplés.* The lyrics were poetic stories delivered with the appropriate emotion. The voice was as important as the lyrics and the most famed singers, such as Andrée Vivianne and Lola Membrives also applied their vocal skills to tangos;

- the male operatic tenors and baritones from the operas whose voices were more important than the lyrics. The Italians Enrique Caruso and Titta Ruffo did not record tangos but created the international appetite for their style of vocal delivery and they unmistakably influenced

> young singers like Carlos Gardel, Alberto Gómez, and Charlo[67].

The obvious expectation from a book dealing with the history of tango singers is to discover who was the first tango singer. Despite many researchers/authors making various claims the truth is that there was no 'first' because there was no such thing as a tango singer. An actress from the theatre who also sang, or even recorded, a tango as part of a much wider repertoire of other genres cannot be described as a tango singer. The Argentinian singers of tangos were not known as tango singers at the time but as simply singers of national songs (up until at least the 1920s).

When we listen today to the recordings of singers from the 1900s we find their voices to be less than easy on the ears. We might dismiss them as poor singers and wonder why anybody could have enjoyed listening to the records in their homes. I have already mentioned above (see *Recordings*) that the technical capabilities, although near miraculous at the time, demanded particular vocal qualities to successfully transfer to the cylinder or disc. The phonographers (those that transferred sound on to a physical object just as photographers did with sight) realised that in order to rise above the sound of the accompanying instrument(s) the voice had to be loud with clear diction and at a certain pitch. Just as some people are more photogenic than others then clearly some singers were more phonogenic. That vocal delivery is not always comfortable for modern ears as many male singers sound as if they were shouting and the women were piercingly shrill sopranos. From the start of the 1930s the technology of the electrical microphone enabled the singer to truly sing in a less projected voice and thereby to become more expressive and more intimate with the listener.

[67] who later turned their vocal skills to the tango genre

The Payadors

The payador is described as a wandering troubadour from the gaucho world. That is an image that creates a perception of musical simplicity whereas the successful payadors were intelligent, creative, and witty[68]. Their art form, the payada, could be performed solo or as a duo (known as *contrapunta*) with each responding to the other in quick-witted rhyming verse, like a vocal duel. They were highly regarded by all strata of society and feted by leading figures in politics and the arts. Historians of the payadors identify their Golden Age as being between 1890 and 1915 during which time they enjoyed high celebrity status in the circus, theatres, and record industry. The payadors spoke their verses with a cadence to emphasise the rhymes and the addition of their guitar turned the recital in to a song but they were not really singers as we understand the term today.

Tango historians often portray payadors as fore-runners of the tango singer and there are lyrics of several later and well-known tangos that pay respect to the payadors by acknowledging their role in preparing the ground for the coming tango pioneers. Perhaps most famous amongst them is the 1944 tango recording by Aníbal Troilo *Café de los Angelitos*[69] in which the chorus opens with 'Café de los Angelitos, bar de Gabino y Cazón' and also praises the voice of Betinotti. I include a short pen portrait of Gabino Ezeiza, Higinio Cazón, and José Betinotti below.

Interestingly, despite the weight of appreciation given to payadors by tango historians the most comprehensively written history of the payadors requires absolutely no mention of tango. Their art form had little or nothing to do with tango except for a few limited

---

[68] the *payada* was an improvised verse on any subject whether personal melancholy, national patriotism, cynical observation of corrupt authorities, or whatever theme often randomly suggested by members of the audience

[69] when the payadors played there it was known as Bar Rivadavia. The name changed to the Angelitos in 1920 and remains today a busy café on the tango tourist trail.

instances. Some did record songs that were, or could be, described as tango but they did not become and were never considered at the time to be tango singers:

- Gabino Ezeiza: *El tango patagones* (1905), *El gaucho* (1912), *Saludo a Paisandú* (1913);
- Higinio Cazón: the tango *El taita* (1905);
- Socrates Figoli: *La Tapera* (1906);
- Florencio Constantino: *La milonga (*1909).

As you would expect there were many notable payadors and there is extensive literature on the subject. I will highlight only a few with links to tango.

Gabino Ezeiza

On 23 July 1884, Gabino Ezeiza was the winner of a high profile payada in Montevideo with the local, and beloved, older payador Juan Nava (father of Arturo, the future tango singer and dancer). After a gruelling competition Ezeiza came through triumphant and such was the public acclaim that the next day the President of Uruguay invited Ezeiza to visit him and his ministers. Even today that date of the 23 July is commemorated every year on both sides of the Río de la Plata as the Day of the Payador. Word of the payadors spread and on 8 December 1885 the Madrid magazine *La Ilustración Española y Americana* published a lengthy article simply entitled 'La Milonga'. The author described the verses of a payador as spontaneous, personal, and sung tenderly from the soul to such an extent that he had seen several hardened gauchos

tearful whilst listening to the milonguero[70]. He referred (as everyone did) to the current milonga star Gabino Ezeiza.

In 1890 at the Victoria Theatre the one act play *Un Día en la Capital* saw its protagonists talk glowingly about the payador Gabino Ezeiza and he was again named and celebrated in 1895 in *El Testamento Ológrafo*. Ezeiza was portrayed in the 1950 film *El Ultimo Payador (The Last Payador)* in a circus tent performing his 1895 composition *Saludo a Paysandu.* You may detect similarities in its melody with that of the tango *Cara Sucia.* You can listen to Gabino himself on his 1913 recording - the words being a clear tribute to the bravery of those rebels fighting at the town of Paysandu.

<u>José Betinotti</u>

In 1898 José Betinotti sang and played guitar at a city circus where he impressed the now senior figure of Gabino Ezeiza who flattered Betinotti with the title El Negro, although Betinotti was quite obviously the son of white Italian immigrants. You can watch a version of that encounter in the 1950 film *El Ultimo Payador* that also includes other interesting moments in the Argentina music business at the start of the 1900s. One scene shows Betinotti singing and playing guitar in front of several large acoustic horns, each agitating a needle that in turn was etching a separate disc. Betinotti made over 100 recordings that included the 1913 *Mi pobre madre querida, Cívica Radical* (named after the political party for

[70] the singers of milongas were described as 'milongueros' - a term that is used today to mean those that regularly attend the social dances known as milongas or dance in a particular way.

the working classes), and his vals compositions *Qué me habrán hecho tus ojos* and *Tu diagnóstico.* The latter is known today thanks to the 1941 version by Ánibal Troilo with singer Francisco Fiorentino. Unfortunately Betinotti did not survive long enough to make any closer transition to the coming world of tango because in 1915 aged 36 he died of alcohol poisoning.

Higinio Cazón

Also influential at that time was Higinio Cazón, like Ezeiza a black Argentinian urban payador born in the barrio of San Telmo. In 1903 a couple of Cazón's songbooks were published and within them were tributes not only to his fellow payadors but also to Juan Bergamino, composer of the tango *Joaquina*. Between 1904 and 1907 one of Cazón's regular venues was a small hut at the back of a bar in the barrio of Almagro operated by his friends Ángel and Luisa Maffia. On more than one occasion he noticed their five-year-old son Pedro had sneaked from his bed to listen to his songs. Within a couple of decades that same Pedro Maffia changed the course of how the bandoneón was played in tango music and became the creative force in the innovative De Caro tango orchestra.

From 1905 to 1909 Cazón recorded many tracks on different labels in Buenos Aires, including the tango *El taita*. When we listen today we must remember that singers were required to project loudly and clearly in to the receiving horn and the resulting, often metallic, reproduction did not accurately reflect their live performances.

Ángel Villoldo

Ángel Gregorio Ghigiola Roggio was born on 16 February 1861 in central Buenos Aires. In about 1902, already a prolific writer of articles and songs, he adopted the *nom de plume* of Villoldo, one of several names used over the years. Today Ángel Villoldo is nearly always described as the Father of Tango that leads to the general assumption that either he created the tango music genre or that he was the most prolific and influential pioneer. It is revealing to discover that he was not known as such during his lifetime. One entry in a catalogue of recordings (by the Casa Tagini) did call him the 'papá of tango criollo' as a promotion for his recordings but that epithet did not stick at the time. On 1 December 1906 the Buenos Aires magazine *Caras y Caretas* published his photograph and described him as the author of a collection of national aires. To Villoldo and to the general public tango was indistinguishable from any other national creole aire. In a 1916 book entitled *Cantos Populares Argentinos* (a compilation of 38 of his song lyrics that included many tangos) he is described by the publisher simply as 'the known Argentine author and composer'. In 1919 his obituary was a summary of his life's achievements and it made no mention of the illustrious 'Father of Tango' title nor in fact of tango, saying only that his compositions were 'genuinely criollo'.

Ángel's talent lay not in his music nor his voice but in his lyrics. He wrote comic, satirical verses and was the equivalent of a music hall, vaudeville, or variety act performer. He was not a trained musician and could neither write nor read musical notation but he had taught himself to strum the guitar and for extra entertainment he blew in to a harmonica mounted on a frame around his neck. Although he was not yet anywhere near describable as a tango performer he was the composer of some of the most successful tangos of the early 1900s many of which (such as *El choclo*, *El porteñito*, *El esquinazo*, *Una fija* and *Cuidado con los cincuenta*[71]) were later recorded in the 1930s to 1950s by the main tango dance orchestras and as a result are still enjoyed by today's tango fans. The modern commentator's appetite to attach lewd meaning to early tangos has established a phallic association with *El choclo*. Villoldo himself said that it was merely about a corn cob that was one of his favourite foods, and he did reference it as a food in other lyrics. His sister, Irene, said that 'El choclo' was the nickname of a friend of the Villoldo family who got the name because his head and hair resembled a corn cob (being long faced with short stubbly blonde hairs). The lyrics seem to be reassuring his friend, who felt humiliated, that actually a 'choclo' was a wonderful thing and was therefore a compliment. Undoubtedly the titillating (posthumously applied) double-entendre will continue to be repeated.

It was in 1903 that Villoldo's compositions started to appeal to the more discerning music-loving society of Buenos Aires helped by the subterfuge of his friend José Luis Roncallo. Roncallo had his own rondalla (a sextet of stringed instruments) and was contracted to play at the refined Café Americano whose proprietor did not approve of tangos. My guess is that he had never heard tangos played in the cafés of La Boca and San Telmo but his mind was made up - he did not approve. To keep the proprietor and his customers comfortable Roncallo chose a safe repertoire of vals, polka, gavota, and marches but into the printed schedule on 7

[71] Villoldo also wrote the lyrics but today his tangos are mainly heard as instrumentals

February 1903 he introduced a new 'danza criolla[72]'. Roncallo's danza criolla was in fact Villoldo's tango *El choclo*. The proprietor and the assembled guests of course found the melody delightfully acceptable. You can hear Villoldo himself performing *El choclo* in 1907[73] and it is undoubtedly less sophisticated than how the instrumental version would have been played by Roncallo at the Café Americano. You can also listen to Villoldo singing, whistling and playing *El choclo* on guitar on an undated Columbia disc, the label of which described him modestly as a 'Popular Artist'. The sheet music for *El choclo* travelled to Europe and became the musical representation of everything that is Argentina to such an extent that it was frequently mistaken for the national anthem.

A Zonophone disc was released in 1905 with Villoldo singing his composition *El porteñito*, today a well-known tango thanks to many later recordings. The label described it not as a tango but simply a popular Argentine song performed by Villoldo, a baritone. Happily both the audio and the image of the label are available to enjoy on the DAHR website[74]. In January 1906 the music retailer Casa Tagini advertised its new arrivals of 'Discos Criollos' on the Columbia label including 28 by Ángel Villoldo within which were the most sought-after tangos: *Bartolo tenia una flauta; Tomá mate ché; El queco; Ensalada criolla;* and *Tango de Negros.*
There is a much-repeated, inaccurate, story[75] about the origins of the composition of *La Morocha,* now a familiar tango but in 1906/07 it was originally recorded as a Spanish tiplé. Villoldo is credited with writing the lyrics in early 1906 and so I was surprised

---

[72] a perfectly respectable musical genre that had been around for decades. In 1859 a Spanish visitor to Argentina wrote about the ever-present and irresistible danza criolla being a mix of the Spanish contradanza with a taste of the Cuban habanera

[73] many sources say1909 which is when it may have become available for sale but the master recording notes say 1907

[74] Discography of American Historical Recordings https://adp.library.ucsb.edu/

[75] see *Pianists/Saborido* below

when I turned to page 31 of the magazine *Caras y Caretas* (11 March 1905) to read the verses of a poem entitled *La morocha* written by the folk and tango poet Francisco Aníbal Riu, a friend and colleague of Villoldo. Not only is the title the same but the specific words and structural style bear more than a striking resemblance to Villodo's later lyrics. My conclusion is that despite having been credited as such for over a century Villoldo cannot be said to have created the words of *La morocha*, one of his most famous and best-selling tangos.

Another much repeated, therefore widely accepted, story says that Villoldo travelled to Paris between 1907 and 1909 together with Alfredo and Flora Gobbi in order to make recordings. Investigators from the Instituto Argentino del Tango have not found any evidence relating to Villoldo's travel to, nor stay in, Europe, neither recording nor performing there, not even holidaying there. Although absence of evidence does not prove an event did not happen it sits in stark contrast with the plentiful evidence relating to the Gobbis in Paris at that time.

In Buenos Aires in December 1907 Villoldo recorded nearly 20 tracks that included several tangos. All of his renditions were in the music hall variety style - fast and light hearted and although regarded as a model Buenos Aires creole artist he was not at all deterred by the unmistakeable Spanish flavour of the castanets. Villoldo additionally recorded under different names such as Arroyo and Navarro as a marketing ploy by the record companies to appear to have a wider range of artists. In 1909 he recorded a tango *La bicicleta* on which his comic singing is accompanied by the tango pioneer pianist Manuel Campoamor, and an unknown percussionist on castanets. It was a tango andaluz version (specifically called a tango cádiz) that had previously been recorded on a cylinder in 1900 by the singer Holber but in order to present it as a local tango Villoldo had added a few Buenos Aires locations (Avenida de Mayo and Palermo). 1909 was the same year that bandoneonist Vicente Greco made the first recordings of an orquesta típica and the contrast of tango styles is extreme. Listen to and compare the 1909 recordings of Villodo's *La bicicleta* and Greco's *Don Juan.* In 1910 Villoldo recorded his tango composition *El torito* that we know today thanks to the 1939 recording of Edgardo Donato. It is always an interesting exercise to listen to the similarities and differences of versions through the years. The Argentinian pianola collector Horacio Asborno has produced a wonderful collection of tangos on his YouTube Channel where you can hear renditions and imagine yourself to be in the café bars of the early 1900s and so I invite you to listen in particular to his pianola version of Villoldo's *El porteñito.*

Villoldo continued to perform and record in to the next decade but died in 1919. He had composed over 100 tangos only some of which remain favourites in today's milongas, due to the recordings of later orchestras:

- *Cuidado con las cincuenta* recorded by Carlos Di Sarli (1942, 1954);
- *El choclo* recorded by almost everyone including Orquesta Típica Victor (1929), Francisco Canaro (1937, 1948), Juan D'Arienzo (1937, 1948, 1954, 1963), Osvaldo Fresedo (1939), Roberto Firpo (1940), Ángel D'Agostino (1941), Carlos Di Sarli (1954);
- *El esquinazo* by Juan D'Arienzo (1938), Roberto Firpo (1939), Francisco Canaro (1951);
- *El porteñito* by Orquesta Típica Victor (1928), Juan D'Arienzo (1938), Francisco Canaro (1941), Ángel D'Agostino (1943), Roberto Firpo (1951);
- *El torito* by Edgardo Donato (1939), Francisco Canaro (1950), Juan D'Arienzo (1954); and
- *Yunta brava* by Juan D'Arienzo (1939).

Alfredo and Flora Gobbi

Alfredo Eusebio Gobbi Chiapapietra was born in Uruguay in 1877 and became known as the entertainer, and later tango composer and recording artist, Alfredo Gobbi. He also became the father of another Alfredo Gobbi, the 1950s tango violinist, orchestra leader, composer and recording artist.

Gobbi senior joined the famous Anselmo Circus in Buenos Aires in 1895 and in 1900 travelled with the Argentinian Petray Brothers circus troupe to Europe in its presentation of *Juan Moreira.* When he returned from Europe Alfredo toured the Argentina provinces in 1905 where he met and married the Chilean born soprano singer Flora Hortensia Rodríguez. The two formed a singing duo known as Los Gobbis[76]. In early July 1906 they were in London recording creole songs that included *La morocha.* They sailed to North America and in the Victor Philadelphia laboratories during a two-week period in July and August they recorded over 50 creole songs from Argentinian composers Arturo Navas, Nemesio Trejo, Antonio Reynoso, Enrique García Velloso, Gabino Ezeiza, Alfredo Bevilacqua, Rosendo Mendizábal, and Ángel Villoldo. Those that are still familiar to today's tango fans, due to recordings by later orchestras, were *El porteñito, La morocha, Apolo, and Reina de Saba.* In December 1907 Gobbi was in Buenos Aires being recorded by the visiting Victor engineer Bill Nafey. There are accounts of the Gobbis being in both Buenos Aires and Paris during the same years, which appears to be contradictory but it is more than possible that they travelled several times between the two[77]. In July 1909 the specialist trade magazine *Talking Machine World* published an article with a photograph of Alfredo and Flora Gobbi saying that the Edison Company had brought them 'at

---

[76] and also as Los Campos

[77] the average sailing time across the Atlantic was 20 days

great expense' to New York to make recordings, that they had already travelled to Spain and France and were contracted to imminently return to Italy. The Gobbis were, it said, acknowledged as the best singers of popular song from the latest plays and they performed in a quaint gaucho style. It clarified that Alfredo Gobbi was not a real gaucho but a man of refinement with an intense love of the customs and traditions of the gaucho song. The Gobbis recorded extensively both solo and as a duet, mainly supported by an orchestra, but Alfredo also recorded 16 songs accompanied only by guitar.

When the Gobbis were in Paris they recorded Villoldo's comic song *Cuidado con los 50*, *El criollo falsificado* (being the same melody as *El porteñito)*, and *Cariño puro* (the same melody as *El choclo*). Alfredo also put lyrics to Ernesto Ponzio's *Don Juan* and recorded it as *Mozos guapos*. Additionally Alfredo's own compositions, for example *A mi manis*, were recorded on the Gath & Chaves label by the Band of the Paris Republican Guard. The Gobbis recorded so prolifically (both individually and as a duet, on cylinders and discs, and for many different labels in the USA, Europe, and Argentina) that they became known as the 'Kings of the Gramophone'. It is worthy of note that the majority of their record labels describe the songs simply as 'Criollo' even though today we describe many of them as tango. In contrast, in 1911 Alfredo Gobbi's songs were recorded by the Buenos Aires Municipal Band and were described on the labels not as criollo but as tango. This is because the band's instrumental was for dancing (hence 'tango') whilst Gobbi's vocals were not (hence 'criollo' or 'nacional aire').

After 1910 Alfredo continued to entertain but at nothing like the pace nor received acclaim that he had experienced in the previous decade. He tried to adapt to the new sounds of tango and in 1914 as the leader of the Orquesta Típica Criollo Porteño (a quartet of bandoneón, violin, flute, and guitar) he recorded instrumental tangos of Roberto Firpo, Vicente Loduca, and Carlos Macchi. In

1924 he released two comic songs in his old familiar style, both of which were accompanied by the tango orchestra of Roberto Firpo, and in 1926 he appeared on stage with the tango duo Agustín Irusta and Roberto Fugazot.

We will not hear more about 'Los Gobbis' so will say farewell now. Alfredo died in 1938 and his widow Flora lived long enough to see their son, Alfredo Junior, flourish. Alfredo Gobbi Junior had grown up in the world of tango entertainment, he had learnt to play violin, and in his early twenties accompanied budding tango stars such as Osvaldo Pugliese, Aníbal Troilo, and Pedro Laurenz. For today's tango fans, and internet search engines, the name 'Alfredo Gobbi' is the son who became known as the 'Romantic Violin of Tango', directed his own tango orchestra, and made recordings from 1947 to 1957. Alfredo Senior and his wife Flora, the prolific pioneer tango performers and recording artists who were bestowed with the title 'Kings of the Gramophone', are nearly forgotten.

Arturo Navas

Both Arturo Navas and his father Juan de Nava were composers, lyricists, and performers. Arturo recorded nearly 30 tracks in December 1907 and went on to record 100 more over the next 10 years, several of which were his father's compositions and lyrics. Listen to Arturo's *El carretero* recorded in Buenos Aires on 28 December 1907. The label did not identify the song as a tango but you may find the melody familiar. Listen now to the popular tango *Zaraza* recorded by Ignacio Corsini and by Francisco Canaro with singer Charlo (both 1929) and then by Rodolfo Biagi with singer Jorge Omar (1941). The melodies are the same and the lyrics also included the words 'buey zaraza' and 'huella'. Now listen to the recording of *Huella buey* by the Orquesta Típica Victor (1929). The nephew of *Huella buey's* composer confirmed that the melody, theme, and lyrics had been taken directly from the Navas 1907 creole song *El carretero*. These comparisons remind us that many of the tangos that we hear and enjoy today have their origins in the work of the earlier pioneers who are now largely unknown and certainly unappreciated. The same pioneers of course had themselves built upon the handed down melodies and themes of earlier generations whose names and works are now beyond retrieval.

Arturo Navas remained in the entertainment business and developed a friendship with singer Carlos Gardel who recorded several of his compositions. We can see Navas in a 1930 film clip, with sound, introducing Gardel who sang *El carretero*.

Arturo's recordings include *Tango de los negros* (1907), *Ensalada Criolla* (1910) from the creole play of that name, and *Saludo a Paysandú* (1911) that, if speeded up, is largely the same melody as the tango *Cara Sucia.*

Women Singers

The story of tango musicians from the earliest times through to the 1940s is predominantly a male story with the role of women generally being as singers from the non-dance world of theatre, cabaret and film[78].

There was nothing new about female star singers in the Buenos Aires theatre and they were amongst the first local artists to record

[78] of course there are exceptions

on discs in the city. In 1902 the first sung tango recorded in Buenos Aires was Villoldo's composition *La bicicleta* performed by actress Eloísa Ceballos. It was already a popular comic song and was delivered in the usual tango andaluz style. In 1903 to 1905 the visiting French songstress Andhrée[79] Vivianne starred at the Buenos Aires theatres of the Casino and the Royal bringing the best of the songs from the trendy French capital. She particularly delighted her audiences with her spell-binding renditions of songs from the Pampas. Although French she soon became an honorary criolla and from 1904 to early 1909 recordings were released of her singing hits from the Buenos Aires theatre. In 1905 she recorded the tango *El porteñito* (although her lyrics were adapted to *La porteñita*) on a cylinder and the same tango on both Odeón and Zonophone discs in 1907. Her soprano voice is not the singing technique associated with tango today but it was nevertheless delivered in the desired style of its time. This is how tango arrived within the broader population - not explosively as a new and unfamiliar form performed by a new wave of avant-garde artists but via the familiar artists of the day in their familiar genre whether folk, stringed ensembles, theatrical pieces, comic songs, or brass bands. Tango was performed in accordance with everyone's diverse taste.

In a similar soprano voice, on 23 July 1906, Flora Hortensia Rodríguez de Gobbi recorded Villoldo's tango *El porteñito* supported by an orchestra and in that same year she sang the same tune in a duet with her husband Alfredo Gobbi but it was entitled *El criollo falsificado*. It was not uncommon during those years to find songs with the same melody but different lyrics and title. During the following two weeks she made over 50 recordings released on the Victor label, being a mixture of solos and duets.

---

[79] known in Argentina as Andrée without the 'h'

Ermelinda Spinelli was born in Italy in 1880 and became the actress Linda Thelma (right) when she completely adopted the accent and creole characteristics of Buenos Aires. In 1907 she recorded a variety of songs including the tango *La morocha.* Similarly in 1909 she recorded different genres that included Villoldo's tangos *El pechador* and *El caprichoso.* Her vocal style is not particularly attractive to today's tango fans but she was recorded because she was a star of the day. In 1912 she travelled to Spain where she sang tangos not in the andaluz style but with a distinctly creole (and specifically porteña) delivery. In 1915 the Buenos Aires newspaper *Crítica* praised both her 'italo-criolla' singing and her dance moves dressed in the style of a street compadrito. In 1922 she was contracted to perform in Paris where she stayed until 1926 when the visiting Francisco Canaro included her in his orquesta típica line up and took her on his tour of the USA.

3. Brass Bands

Brass bands were commonly heard in the cities of Argentina. Newspaper reports, sometimes accompanied by photographs, reveal that they played locally in community venues, parks, theatres, and particularly at public celebrations and street parades. The instruments were brass, woodwind, and percussion and notably did not include piano, violin, bandoneón nor double bass[80]. Their repertoire included a wide variety of music from classical to the latest popular tunes, both national and international, including tangos.

The new capabilities to record on cylinders and discs meant that brass bands were natural contenders to provide a taste of Buenos Aires music. They were chosen not only because they were familiar to the general public but because the North American and European recording technicians had already established that the volume projected by brass bands together with the sharp metallic sound of their instruments were ideally suited to the recording process.

As a result, from the first decade of the 1900s we can enjoy dozens

1901 Buenos Aires Police Band

of recordings by bands including the Banda Municipal de la Ciudad de Buenos Aires, Banda de la Policía de la Provincia de Buenos Aires, Banda Italo-Argentina, Banda del Teatro Apolo, Banda del

[80] the signature instruments of the later tango orchestras

Pabellón de las Rosas, Banda del Teatro Nacional, and several Infantry Regiments. Tangos were also recorded by brass bands in Europe and North America such as the Band of the Republican Guard (Paris), the Royal Military Band (London), the Victor Argentine Orchestra and Sousa's Band (Philadelphia/New York). Some of my favourites are:

- *El choclo* recorded by the Victor Argentine Orchestra (a brass band) in the USA (1906);
- *El incendio* recorded by the Banda Italo-Argentina, directed by Antonio Lozzi (1907);
- *Hotel Victoria, El Porteñito* recorded by the Banda de la Policía de Buenos Aires, directed by Antonio Rivara (1907); and
- *El irresistible*, *El choclo, Cosa linda barata* recorded by the Banda Municipal de la Ciudad de Buenos Aires, directed by Arturo De Bassi (1908).

Tango recordings by bands continued in to the next decade. In the carnival months of 1910 and 1912 the Banda de Pabellón de las Rosas, directed by César Sesso, recorded over 125 tracks including tangos (on the Victor label). In 1911 the Buenos Aires Banda Municipal recorded tangos (on the Columbia label) that are all cheerful and thankfully well preserved. In 1913 in the USA Victor recorded North American bands playing tangos:

- the Victor Military Band released *Argentine Tango* labelled 'for dancing at 42 bars per minute' and included castanets;
- the New York Military Band recorded the Eduardo Arolas composition *Una noche de garufa;* and
- the Indestructible Military Band made a cylinder recording of *El irresistible.* It is interesting to compare this with the 1946 version by orquesta típica Rodolfo Biagi.

4. Rondallas

A rondalla was a group of musicians playing a variety of stringed instruments, without brass, piano or bandoneón but sometimes with a flute. Confusingly the term was on occasions used more loosely, for example in 1913 recordings of bandoneonists Augusto Berto, Vicente Greco, and Genaro Espósito, and of pianists Alfredo Bevilacqua and Roberto Firpo were inaccurately advertised as rondallas. String rondallas played and recorded a wide variety of genres and offered a smoother, gentler alternative to the more forceful brass bands. In 1903 the rondalla of José Luis Roncallo introduced the tango *El choclo* as a new creole dance tune to the refined customers of the Café Americano. In 1907 the rondalla of José Vazquez (below) recorded tangos including *Yunta brava* and *Venus* and in 1909 the Rondalla del Gaucho Relampago recorded several tangos including *El caburé.* Also in 1909 the trio of stringed instruments called the Estudiantina Centenario (effectively a rondalla) recorded tangos including: *Hotel Victoria, El esquinazo, and El entrerriano.*

Slippping in to the next decade rondallas continued to record tangos amongst their wider repertoire, such as:

- Rondalla de José Vázquez (shown below) *Hotel Victoria, Joaquina, Z Club* (1913);
- Rondalla del Gaucho Relampago *Una noche de la garufa* (1913);
- Rondalla Atlanta *La pebeta* (1913); and
- Rondalla Criollo Fígaro *Gran Hotel Victoria, Rodríguez Peña, El irresistible* (1913).

Tangos did not belong to any particular sound, style, performer, nor socio-economic class and was often not even described as tango. It is for that reason that tango remains difficult to define and does not fall neatly in to any of the subsequently constructed myths and supposed traditions.

5. Pianists

Alfredo Bevilacqua

On Friday 20 February 1874 the Italian Pedro Bevilacqua and his Uruguayan pregnant wife María boarded the train at Retiro, Buenos Aires, heading 15 kilometres north to Olivos where she was due to give birth. Not long in to the journey, whilst travelling through the barrio of Belgrano, María Bevilacqua was the centre of a commotion in the carriage as she prematurely delivered her son to the world. The unexpected railroad birth of Alfredo Antonio Bevilacqua attracted press attention with one newspaper exposing him as 'The passenger without a ticket'. Among all of the tango stars Alfredo Bevilacqua thereby secured his place in history as the one who achieved fame at the earliest age.

As a young boy Alfredo Bevilacqua learnt how to play the guitar and then the piano and by 1895 the city's census showed him to be 21 years old, with neither parent living, literate, and a piano teacher.

In 1902 he published his tango composition *Venus*, the sheet music of which reads 'Performed to great success at the Teatro Victoria[81]'. It was recorded in 1907 by the string rondalla of José Vázquez, in 1912 by bandoneonist Juan Maglio and in 1913 by Bevilacqua himself. Much later *Venus* was recorded by orchestra leaders Juan D'Arienzo (1944) and by Rodolfo Biagi (1961). In 1903 Bevilacqua composed the tango *Apolo* that although it had lyrics added later, by Ángel Villoldo and Alfredo Gobbi, was mainly played as an instrumental. It was recorded on 25 July 1906 in the USA by the Orquesta Argentina Victor and much later by Roberto Firpo's quartet in 1949.

Bevilacqua was a frequent pianist at the Teatro de Pasatiempo, a

[81] a city centre venue just four blocks from the Plaza de Mayo

regular venue for dancers, and was also a music teacher to many budding tango musicians. In 1904 he was expecting his regular student, the 14-year-old Juan Deamboggio, for his music theory and bandoneón lesson. When Juan arrived, he was accompanied by an older man with whom he worked and who wanted to learn to play the piano. Juan said that he wanted Bevilacqua to teach them jointly so that they could play together. The young man was 20-year-old Roberto Firpo who could not have found a more qualified teacher to put him on the road to becoming the most successful tango pianist over the next 60 years. The young bandoneonist Juan Deamboggio also achieved tango fame - in Paris in the 1920s performing and recording under the better-known name of Bachicha.

In the February/March 1906 carnival both Bevilacqua and his fellow pianist Rosendo Mendizábel directed an orchestra of 20 musicians at the Teatro Marconi. The details of the repertoire are not known but I can imagine them at their pianos thundering out the latest dance tunes, including their own tango compositions.

In 1908 Bevilacqua was at a friend's house and played his recently composed tango (that was later published as *Independencia*). His friend liked it so much that he wanted to hear it again and invited his 8-year-old son, Ángelito, to try it. Bevilacqua was delighted to hear young Ángel D'Agostino play his new work and from then on frequently encouraged the boy with his piano studies. Ángel did continue practicing but at that time he was not at all keen on tango music and much preferred to play the classics[82].

In 1910, the centenary year of the May Revolution, Bevilacqua directed a brass band in the Avenida de Mayo and played his tango *Independencia* during the procession of the President and the visiting Princess Isabel of Spain. He presented her with a signed copy of the

[82] Ángel D'Agostino became the leader of a tango dance orchestra in the 1940s and his recordings are still much-loved today.

music for which he received great praise from the princess and the assembled crowds.

1910 Centenary parade with Princess Isabel of Spain and band lining the path in Plaza de Mayo

Independencia was recorded by bandoneonist Juan Maglio (1912) but is better known to us today by the versions of Juan D'Arienzo (1942, 1953). Sadly Bevilacqua was not able to hear D'Arienzo's punchy renditions as he died six months before the 1942 recording.

Alfredo Bevilacqua also composed the tangos:

- *Emancipación* recorded by Juan Maglio (1912) and decades later by Osvaldo Pugliese (1955); and
- *Gran muñeca* recorded by Genaro Esposito (1914), and his former students Roberto Firpo (1941) and Ángel D'Agostino (1943).

Manuel Campoamor

Born in Montevideo in 1877 and brought up in Buenos Aires, Manuel Campoamor was a talented pianist but not musically trained and so could neither read nor write musical notation. He did however have lessons with tango pianist Rosendo Mendizábal[83]. In 1894 he was playing at dance halls and particularly made his name during the February and March carnivals from 1896 onwards. He had developed a certain swing in his style so much so that the black payador Gabino Ezeiza paid the complement of calling the white-skinned Campoamor El Negro and invited him on tour as his accompanying pianist. In 1899 Campoamor published his tango composition *El Sargento Cabral* that became commercially successful and was one of the first tangos to cross the Atlantic. In 1907 it was recorded in Paris by the Band of the Republican Guard. Sadly it is little known today because it was not among the limited recorded repertoire of the relatively few orchestras whose music is played at today's tango dance events.

In 1901 Campoamor published his composition *La c…ara de la l…una* that he had already made popular as *La concha de la lora*, an unmistakable crudity[84] that the publisher needed to change hence the dots and replacement title. As the more socially acceptable *La cara de la luna* it too became a massive hit in the first decade of the century, and was recorded by bandoneonist Vicente Greco in 1911. Today it is known by the recorded versions by Francisco Canaro (1941) and Juan D'Arienzo (1971).

In 1905 Campoamor was the pianist supporting payador singers Gabino Ezeiza (on the recording of *El cochero*, a milonga) and Higinio Cazón (on the tango *El taita*). On the latter he is most clearly heard in the first and closing 10 seconds, before and after the

---

[83] see below

[84] 'Lora' being a female bird was slang for a woman and a concha is a shell.

distracting voice of Cazón. Also in 1905 he recorded a piano solo of his own composition, the tango *La Franela*. In 1909 he accompanied Ángel Villoldo on the recording of the tango *La Bicicleta*.

Campoamor gave up composing in 1905 saying that the time had come for him to step aside as the new generation had gripped the public's attention by creating a different tango rhythm. We should pause to think of 1905 as being the new tango generation. His description of the change in tango style coincides with the 1903 article in *Caras y Caretas* declaring that the hitherto familiar tango was dying[85]. To understand better his style of tango listen to his 1911 piano rendition of the well-known tango *Joaquina* and then compare it with the recording in the same year by Vicente Greco followed by the more familiar versions by Juan D'Arienzo (1935) and Francisco Canaro (1939). Today's tango fans will be attracted more to the latter two but in the 1890s to 1910 Campoamor was an exciting, much sought after sensation.

Despite his talent and enthusiasm for tango Manuel Campoamor did not commit economically to a life as a musician but was in almost continuous full-time employment, a couple of decades of which was in the accounting office of the Gath and Chaves department store. He died in contented retirement in 1941.

His other tango compositions include:

- *La metralla* recorded by Francisco Canaro (1945); and
- *En el séptimo cielo* recorded by Francisco Canaro (1954).

[85] see page 14

Arturo De Bassi

Cayetano De Bassi was a professional musician and bandleader and when he became a father, in the 1880s and 1890s, he wasted no time in giving musical instruction to his sons Antonio, Tomas, and Arturo. All subsequently became musicians and composers of popular tunes in the theatre. However it was the compositions of Arturo that would become most familiar to tango dancers.

At the age of 10 Arturo was standing surrounded by the adults of his father's band as he played the clarinet. Five years later he had graduated to playing the piano in the orchestra of the famous Podestá theatre company. The orchestra director was the renowned Antonio Reynoso who came to fame in 1897 with the play *Justicia Criolla,* now credited with being the first successful theatre production of a tango danced in a conventillo setting.

In 1906, aged 16, Arturo De Bassi composed the tango *El incendio*. Reynoso liked it so much that he invited Arturo to play it at the theatre but only during the interval. Following its enthusiastic reception Reynoso then included it in his orchestra's repertoire. *El incendio* soon became De Bassi's first great success and its opening notes came easily and readily to the lips of the whistling population. It went on to be recorded in 1908 by the Banda Italo-Argentina and in 1911 by Vicente Greco but it is better known to us today by the versions of Rodolfo Biagi (1938), Carlos Di Sarli (1940, 1951), and Alfredo Gobbi Junior (1948).

Following his success with *El incendio*, in 1908 Arturo De Bassi confidently submitted his latest tango to a competition, organised by the newspaper *Ultima Hora*, but was shocked when the judges dismissed it at the early stages. Indignant, he paid for the sheet music to be published and on the front page declared in underlined capital letters its dismal failure in the competition[86]. Such a bold and unorthodox line of advertising attracted attention resulting in it becoming a best seller. It was subsequently recorded in 1912 by the star bandoneonist Juan Maglio. We still enjoy that tango, *La catrera,* today through the versions of Juan D'Arienzo (1938, 1949, 1955, 1963), Alfredo Gobbi Junior (1951), and Héctor Varela (1957).

In 1908 De Bassi was leading the Banda Municipal de la Ciudad de Buenos Aires and their repertoire was heavily weighted in favour of tangos. The band recorded at least 20 tangos that year including some of those still known today (thanks to the recordings of later orchestras): *Cosa linda barata, El irresistible,* and *El otario.*

Arturo De Bassi went on to compose many more tangos, to lead orchestras, make tango recordings, and become a leading theatre producer.

Roberto Firpo

The name of Roberto Firpo, born in 1884, became synonymous with tango music from the 1910s despite him being a late developer. Before that in 1903 he was working in a steel mill where he met Juan Deamboggio. As we have read above the two of them took regular lessons with Alfredo Bevilacqua. In order to practice the theory that he had learnt from Bevilacqua Roberto Firpo went home and made his own instrument from glass bottles each with specific amounts of water to achieve the musical scale, more or less. A year or so later he was at the piano entertaining customers in a bar in the port of Bahía Blanca and in 1907 returned to Buenos Aires to play piano in

[86] *Tango no premiado en el Concurso de Ultima Hora* (Not awarded a prize at the *Ultima Hora* competition)

duets, trios, and quartets with his friend Deamboggio on bandoneón and clarinettist Juan Carlos Bazán.

It was in a trio with Bazán, and violinist Federico Laféмina, that he played at the city cycle track, the Velódromo, that had closed in 1908 but was thereafter licenced for the playing of music after midnight. Whilst there Firpo composed a tango and dedicated it to a dancer - Manuela López, an alluring woman armed and adept with a knife. Her wealthy lover paid Firpo well for the rights to his tango *La Gaucha Manuela*[87]. Five years later in 1912 the bandoneonist Juan Maglio recorded *La Gaucho Manuela* so we can hear a reasonably contemporary version of Firpo's composition (although without piano). Standing at the Velódromo entrance Bazán used to play a calling tune on his clarinet in order to attract customers. So attractive was the call that the Velódromo started to take many of the customers from the nearby Restaurant Tarana[88] until the latter's owner made a greater financial offer to the trio, who obligingly changed locations. A musical reference to the beguiling tune can be heard at the start of Bazán's now famous composition *La chiflada* perhaps best-known today by the versions of Francisco Canaro (1941) and by Ángel D'Agostino (1942).

Roberto Firpo went on to record in the trio of Genaro Esposito in 1912 and within a couple of years dominated the tango scene becoming a prolific composer and performer, and by recording almost continuously until 1959.

[87] Firpo later used phrasing from that tango to improve the half-written marching tune by Gerardo Matos Rodríguez called *La cumparsita*

[88] also known as the Café Hansen

Rosendo Mendizábal

The pianist Anselmo Rosendo Cayetano Mendizábal, born in 1868, is always described as Afro-Argentinian in a way that infers (or directly asserts) the African links to tango music. It is true that he was black-skinned. His grandfather, also Rosendo Mendizábal, was a respectable member of the Buenos Aires establishment: a member of the Grand Lodge of Masons, a master of art, editor of the magazine *El Porteño*, and married in to a wealthy ranch-owning family. His father, Horacio, was a published author of romantic poetry. There is no evidence to suggest that young Rosendo was exposed to any African cultural nor musical heritage.

The most eye-catching story is that he was the regular pianist at the dance salon of María La Vasca where he kept everyone happy and dancing with his repertoire of popular tunes including his latest tango composition *El entrerriano*. The cover of the sheet music (shown) appears in tango books and tango websites and is always declared to be dated 1897 and the 'first published tango'. However, that is a story - there is no evidence to date the composition nor its debut. The investigator (and president of the Instituto del Tango, Buenos Aires) Marcelo Castello has proven beyond doubt that this particular sheet music was published no earlier than 1913. The dateline of Maria La Vasca and her link to tango is similarly unproven. Rosendo is also frequently described as the resident pianist at another renowned dance salon - Lo de Laura - but again there is no direct evidence of that.

We do know that:

- he did compose *El entrerriano* under his pseudonym of Anselmo Rosendo;
- in the February/March 1906 carnival both Mendizábel and Alfredo Bevilacqua dually directed a 20-piece orchestra;
- in September 1906 a play at the Teatro Royal included a number of his tango compositions;
- the tango pianist and composer Enrique Saborido said that he was inspired by Mendizábal who was unique in the way that he used his left hand on the bass notes - a description that brings to mind the deep throbbing bass notes and arrastres[89] of later tango pianists Carlos Di Sarli and Osvaldo Pugliese.

Mendizábal's tango compositions include:

- *El entrerriano* recorded in 1911 by the Buenos Aires Municipal Band but we are more familiar with the later versions recorded by the Orquesta Típica Victor (1927), Francisco Canaro (1927 and 1952), Roberto Firpo (1937), Rodolfo Biagi (1941), Osvaldo Fresedo and Aníbal Troilo (both in 1944), and Juan D'Arienzo (1946 & 1954). *El entrerriano* was also played by the orchestra of Ernesto Ponzio and Juan Carlos Bazán in the first Argentinian-made film with sound *Tango* in 1933;
- *Don José María* recorded by the Spanish Band (1906), Juan Maglio (1912), Genaro Esposito (1914), and then revived with enthusiasm by Carlos Di Sarli (1930, 1943, 1952 & 1954);
- *Viento en popa* was recorded by Juan Maglio (1912), Genaro Esposito (1914), Francisco Canaro (1937), and Roberto Firpo (1948);
- *Z Club* recorded in the USA by the Victor Argentine Orchestra (1906), in Buenos Aires by the Orchestra of the

[89] a dragging or strumming effect

Theatre Apolo (1908) and the Banda Italo-Argentina (1910), and in Paris by the Band of the Republican Guard (1909). Thereafter it seems to have disappeared until revived by Roberto Firpo (1942); and

- *Reina de Saba* recorded by the Victor Argentine Orchestra in 1906 and the Banda Española in 1907 but more familiarly by Francisco Canaro (1941) and Roberto Firpo (1949).

Mendizábel, in order to support his growing family of 7 children, supplemented his income by giving piano lessons at the homes of wealthy families and continued to entertain wherever and whenever he could. The last story of his life is that he was invited to play at a local café but, as it did not have a piano, he took along his guitar when mid-performance he slumped in his chair and died. His death certificate declared his death in 1913, aged 45, due to kidney failure.

Carlos Posadas

It is commonly suggested that there are African roots to the tango compositions of Carlos Posadas. Such claims are made simply based on his dark skin colour. The Posadas family background and the environment of Carlos' youth firmly orientated him to European culture. His parents[90] were sufficiently wealthy to send their oldest son Manuel to Brussels in 1879 in order to study classical music for three years. When Manuel returned to Buenos Aires he was featured in *La Tribunal Nacional* (12 September 1882) as an outstanding violinist. He was only 19 years old and barely known and so I suspect that his father had sufficient social standing to exert the necessary influence on the newspaper. Being classically trained Manuel was

[90] Manuel Posadas and Emilia Smit

not only adept on the violin, in 1886 he advertised his services as a piano instructor and in 1890 as a teacher of music. Manuel taught his younger brother Carlos (born in 1874) how to read music and how to play guitar, violin and piano - all presumably in his own classical style. Manuel's full-time employment was in theatre orchestras, most notably at the Teatro Politeama where he introduced Carlos in to the theatrical world.

Carlos Posadas grew in to a talented musician of many instruments, he played in orchestras ranging from classical to the mass-market theatre, and was a regular orchestra leader at the annual carnivals. In February 1909 he directed the orchestra of 30 music teachers at the Teatro de la Avenida supporting a visiting French Can-Can troupe. In 1910 he moved to the Teatro Marconi and made that his regular carnival venue for the rest of his life.

Over the years he worked with tango composers, such as bandoneonist Juan Maglio, to transcribe their tunes on to paper thereby enabling the production of saleable music sheets. He also mixed and became friends with many other rising stars of the tango world:

- violinist Ernesto Zambonini dedicated to Posadas his most famous tango composition *La clavada* (today we know Osvaldo Fresedo's 1933 recording); and
- pianist Juan Bergamino, the composer of the tango *Joaquina*, was the godfather of Posadas' son.

Carlos Posadas is most of all remembered for his own tango compositions, of which there were over fifty. As is often the case with the pioneers their most popular tangos at the time are no longer familiar, simply because they were not amongst the few recordings that are available to us today. Those that have been preserved on record for 21st century dancers include:

- *El retirao* recorded by Francisco Canaro (1927), Carlos Di

Sarli (1939), and Aníbal Troilo (1957);

- *El jaguel* recorded by Francisco Canaro (1927), Carlos Di Sarli (1943, 1953 and 1956), and Juan D'Arienzo (1967);
- *El tamango* recorded by Aníbal Troilo (1941) and Juan D'Arienzo (1967); and
- *Cordón de oro* recorded by Aníbal Troilo (1941), Enrique Rodriguez (1945), and Juan D'Arienzo (1967).

In 1918, the year that Carlos Posadas died, he was playing for a zarzuela company in the Teatro Avenida and alongside him was the 17-year-old violinist Juan D'Arienzo. Neither could have realised the symbolic significance of their joint performance - the early pioneer and the later disrupter of tango dance music.

Enrique Saborido

Born in 1877[91] Enrique Saborido moved with his Spanish parents as a small child from Montevideo to Buenos Aires where he learnt to play the violin before changing to the piano. One of his early teachers was tango pioneer Rosendo Mendizábal. Although Saborido earned his money by playing at private functions in the homes of the wealthy his preference was for tango in the dance halls. From 1899 he formed his own groups comprising guitar, violin, harp and flute and his fellow musicians included violinist Genaro Vázquez and flautist Vicente Pecci, who themselves were core musicians in a number of pioneering tango bands.

Saborido, in various interviews decades after the events, told the story of his most famous composition *La morocha*. His memories are

[91] although some sources claim 1885

not entirely reliable in terms of specific dates nor the order of events however in an interview published in *Caras y Caretas* 9 January 1928 he did tell an entertaining tale. He was playing as the regular pianist in the Bar Reconquista and one evening in 1906 he was challenged by the singer and dancer, Lola Candales, to produce a song for her by the following morning. That night between 5am and 6.30am he produced a tune but could not come up with the words for her to sing so he called upon his friend Ángel Villoldo who provided the lyrics by 10am. He named the composition *La Morocha* (the brunette), Lola Candales having had dark hair and complexion. In 1935 Saborido was interviewed by the tango chroniclers Héctor and Luis Bates who in their (often inaccurate) *Historia del Tang*o declared the date of composition to have been 24 December 1905. Saborido said the sheet music, published in 1906, was then transported on the naval training ship *Fragata Sarmiento* to Europe where it was widely distributed and became the start of the tango story in Paris and beyond. The story of *La morocha* has been re-told so many times that it is accepted as fact and some of it may be, however there is evidence that undermines the commonly told tale:

- Saborido is the registered composer but the tune of *La Morocha* is not original. It is a re-worked version of the 1897 tango andaluz *No Me Vengas con Paradas* from the zarzuela play *Gabino El Mayoral.* You can watch a version of this song in the 1939 film *La Vida es un Tango;*

- the label on the 1910 Victor recording by Dolores (Lola) Candales showed her to be the composer and lyricist. She was so associated with the title 'La Morocha' that even today there is a road in Montevideo called 'Dolores Candales La Morocha';

- Ángel Villoldo is credited with the lyrics and yet a poem with the same title and similar words had been published beforehand (11 March 1905) by Francisco Aníbal Riu;

- at the time *La morocha* was not known as a tango. The Columbia label of the 1907 recording by Alfredo and Flora Gobbi made no mention of it as a tango and Flora Gobbi's 1907 solo recording is described as a Spanish tiple;

- its journey to Europe and its status as the first tango sheet music is not as described by Saborido. I examined the naval records of the *Fragata Sarmiento* and it did not sail to Europe in 1906 as Saborido alleges. However in June 1907 the *Sarmiento* did dock at Portsmouth and then Dartmouth in England, moving on to Wilhelmshaven in the Netherlands, then south to Brest and Bordeaux in France, Ferrol in Spain, Lisbon in Portugal, across to Tenerife in the Canary Islands before its return trip across the Atlantic. Although there is no record of a cargo of tango sheet music I am happy to accept that it was this tour that distributed *La morocha* around Europe - and if so it would make Captain José Moneta the most unlikely, and probably unwitting, pioneer promoter of Argentinian tango. Despite Saborido's claims, the sheet music for *La Morocha* was not the start of the proliferation of tango in Europe as there were earlier recordings of other Argentine tangos by bands using sheet music in London and Paris from 1905.

Throughout the following decades *La morocha* gained popularity as an instrumental and was recorded by many orchestras including Juan D'Arienzo (1937, 1949, 1963), Roberto Firpo (1938, 1950), Carlos Di Sarli (1941, 1951, 1954), and Francisco Canaro (1959). In 1929 it was recorded with lyrics, also to great success, by the orchestra of Francisco Canaro and singer Ada Falcón. You can listen, on the YouTube Channel of my friend the pianola specialist

Horacio Asborno, to the recording[92] of *La morocha* by the Banda de la Policía de Buenos Aires played on a Victrola gramophone.

Enrique Saborido's next big hit composition came in 1908 the year after he played it, still unnamed, at a dance hall where it was heard by Felicia Ilarregui, the wife of the influential theatre producer Carlos Pacheco. She was so enthusiastic that Saborido dedicated it to her. The original sheet music included the lyrics written by Felicia's husband but the tango *Felicia* is known to us today as exclusively instrumental and the most familiar recordings are those by Osvaldo Fresedo (1927), Francisco Canaro (1929, 1952), Adolfo Carabelli (1932), Juan D'Arienzo (1939, 1947, 1954, 1963), and Roberto Firpo (1937, 1950).

Saborido became widely known as the 'King of Tango' (a title given to several pioneers in this era) and continued to compose and perform but his passion changed direction towards the dance. He stopped performing in 1908 and opened his own tango dance school, located near today's corner of Santa Fe and Avenida 9 de Julio. He soon became a well-respected dance teacher and was frequently invited to demonstrate at the homes of wealthy clients that led to a prestigious event in 1912 and the start of his (short) international dancing career in Paris.

92 estimated to be in 1910

LA MOROCHA
Tango Criollo
PIANO y CANTO
ENRIQUE SABORIDO

Bandoneonists

The bandoneón became the defining instrument of 20th century tango although in Buenos Aires it was initially known as the 'bandoleón'. Many commentators claim that the instrument was invented in the 1840s by Heinrich Band in Germany who named it after himself. As usual the truth is not so straight-forward.

The technical concept of the instrument is that it is free-reed, meaning a reed that does not strike against another object whilst vibrating. The origin of the free-reed sound is Southeast Asia and first appeared in the west in the late 1700s in the form of a mouth organ. Using the same techniques, on 19 June 1829 the English inventor Charles Wheatsone[93] began his series of patents for an instrument that would soon become known as a concertina. It was a free-reed wind instrument powered by bellows using buttons to produce a note. In the 1830s the German Carl Uhlig also produced a form of concertina, based on the ideas of the 1829 accordion[94], with the intention of creating a fuller sound similar to the church harmonium. In 1849 Carl Zimmerman from Saxony presented his adapted concertina at the Paris Exhibition and the following year the instrument dealer, Heinrich Band, advertised it for sale. Band created alternative button formations but did not claim any ownership of the instrument and knew it as a concertina and never as a bandoneón. Time moved on and Heinrich Band died in 1860 (aged 39) leaving his widow and son to continue in the musical instrument business. Meanwhile Carl Zimmerman had emigrated and sold his business to Ernst Louis Arnold whose son, Alfred Arnold, devised a new button system named after himself as the 'AA' that became, and remains today, the favourite of tango bandoneonists in Argentina. Despite all of

---

[93] earlier in 1821 Wheatstone exhibited his self-playing piano, invented a form of the microphone in 1829 and electric telegraph in 1834.

[94] invented by the Armenian Cyrill Demian living in Vienna

the inventors and developers in the process it was Heinrich Band's name that was attached to the instrument.

Tales of the first appearances of the bandoneón in Argentina vary from one being brought in from Brazil in 1870 by a man known as Bartolo to a later one imported in 1884 by Thomas, the Englishman (that as an Englishman named Thomas I am particularly drawn to). However, more specific evidence is provided in the journal kept by Major Frederich Bion who was among a group of Swiss emigrants sailing for Uruguay in 1862. One of the group members was Herr Schumacher from the town of Sarganz, Switzerland. He was leaving behind his former life as a blacksmith to become a farm owner. He was also a musician and the instrument that he had chosen to bring with him for the long journey to keep his fellow travellers' spirits high was the bandoneón.

It is clear that the concertina/bandoneón was being played in the Río de la Plata region (of Argentina and Uruguay) from the mid-1860s and that by the end of the century it was in the hands of the tango pioneers. The public was familiar with guitars and mandolins, violins, flutes and clarinets but bandoneóns were novel and complicated and therefore the players of the new sound soon became local celebrities. If the trio, quartet or quintet had a public name then it was generally the name of the bandoneonist. Even the ambitious violinist Francisco Canaro took a decade or more to come out of the shadows of bandoneonists such as Augusto Berto and Vicente Loduca.

Eduardo Arolas

In the barrio of Barracas, in 1892, French immigrants Henri Arola and Marguerite Saury named their newly born son both Lorenzo (in the civil register) and Eduardo (in the church baptism record). He became known as Eduardo Arolas. As a child Eduardo was given guitar and mandolin lessons by neighbour Ricardo 'Mochila' González, a tango pioneer (who many years later changed to the bandoneón). By 1904, at the age of 12, Arolas had switched instrument to the concertina and was playing in local cafés alongside his neighbours who had formed a group. Fortunately for him his neighbours happened to include the tango pioneer bandoneonist Arturo Bernstein with his guitarist brother Luis Bernstein, and the guitarist Luciano Ríos. That same year Arolas was teaching the concertina to another neighbour - the older brother of Rosita Quiroga[95] - but one night when they returned at dawn having stayed out all night making music Quiroga's despairing father took an axe to the offending concertina. Young Arolas, although understandably annoyed at the wanton and costly act of vandalism, wisely decided not to challenge the axe-wielding cart driver from La Boca.

In 1909 at the Café Royal, on the corner of Suarez and Necochea in the barrio of La Boca, the musicians Vicente Loduca (bandoneón), Samuel Castriota (piano), and Francisco Canaro (violin) were perched high on the musicians' gallery entertaining

95 who came to fame in the early 1920s as a tango singer

the customers. During their break they joined some friends at a table, amongst them was Eduardo Arolas now a smartly dressed young man of 17 years. In his memoirs Canaro described Arolas as perfectly groomed and his clothes as highly fashionable and colourfully decorated. After a few drinks the group of friends asked that Arolas should be allowed to play so Loduca offered him his bandoneón. Without hesitation Arolas chose his own composition, the tango *Una noche de garufa*. The café customers loved it and so did the trio, so much so that Canaro noted the melody as best as he could for his violin. Later the tango flautist and composer Carlos Hernani Macchi transcribed the tango for piano music enabling it to be published to great commercial success. It remains well-known today thanks to the recordings of Carlos Di Sarli (1931), Ricardo Tanturi (1941), and Francisco Canaro (1953).

Eduardo Arolas was soon given the title 'Tiger of the Bandoneón'. If you listen to tango dance music that was recorded in Buenos Aires between the 1920s and 1950s then it is likely that you will be listening to the influence of Eduardo Arolas as his innovative compositions and style of playing inspired many musicians and composers for decades to come.

Arturo Bernstein

Arturo Bernstein was born in 1882 in Brazil to German parents, Adolfo and Augusta, and was unsurprisingly known as El Aleman (The German). He was considered to be the most skilled of all bandoneonists and further stood out because he could read musical scores whereas most of his bandoneonist peers could not. The pioneer violinist Ernesto Ponzio said that the general rule for identifying the bandoneón player was that if he had music sheets in front of him then it was Bernstein, if not then it was probably Genaro Espósito[96]. Bernstein came to local fame as a solo bandoneonist at the busy Café Royal in the barrio of La Boca in 1903 where he was known not only for having his music sheets in front of him but also beside him a line of waiting beers.

In 1907 he married and began a family meaning that he had to reduce his late-night performances and maintain his income by giving music lessons at home. His many students included:

- the 8-year-old Carlos Marcucci who (literally) became one of the bandoneón virtuosos performing on radio in the 1930s as Los Virtuosos;
- Federico Scorticati who later became the leader of the Orquesta Típica Victor from 1935 to 1941; and
- José Schumacher whose talents were later sought out by Roberto Firpo, Francisco Canaro, and in Paris by Eduardo Bianco and Genaro Espósito.

In the coming decade (1913-1915) Arturo Bernstein would become a recording star performing as El Aleman Quinteto Criolla on the new local Atlanta label.

Vicente Greco

Vicente Greco was born in 1888 in to a home where music and the arts were encouraged, resulting in at least 4 of the 8 children becoming musicians. This 1915 photograph (below) shows Elena (pianist), Vicente (bandoneonist), Domingo (guitarist/singer), and their mother Maria. Ángel Greco, a guitarist, was not at home when the photographer called.

---

[96] we will meet Espósito in *Get To Know the Tango Pioneers 1910 to 1919*

One night Vicente's father, Genaro, and a few friends were playing music late in to the night in the patio of their conventillo when an irate neighbour (who unfortunately for them was also the local policeman) chased them away. To hasten his escape the concertina player abandoned his instrument in to the care of Genaro in

whose home it continued to lie unplayed and inexplicably unclaimed. Vicente eventually brought it down from the top of his parent's wardrobe and soon started taking lessons from another of his father's friends who just happened to be the tango pioneering bandoneonist Sebastián Ramos Mejía[97]. Sebastián recommended to Vicente's parents that they should upgrade him to a bandoneón and in 1902, when he was 14 years old, that is exactly what they did.

Vicente Greco continued with his lessons, started to perform locally, and composed the tango *El pibe* (The Kid). In 1905 unable to write musical notation himself he asked the 10-year-old Carlos Vicente Geroni, already a classically trained pianist[98], to write the musical score for him.

In 1906 Greco went with two friends (playing violin and guitar) on a tour of the Provinces of Buenos Aires and during one performance at a café bar in San Pedro on the usual elevated space (like a theatre box high to the ceiling) all three came tumbling to

---

97 See below in this section

98 Geroni later became a tango convert, sextet leader, and recording artist. See *Get To Know the Tango Pioneers 1910 to 1919* and *1920 to 1935*

the floor as it disintegrated. Some accounts say that the accident left him with a permanent injury to his kidneys that contributed to his early death at the age of 36. But meanwhile he recovered enough to continue playing when (during the months of December 1909 to February 1910) he secured his place in tango history by becoming the first to record tangos as a bandoneonist and the first to be described as an orquesta típica.

Greco had been invited by the gramophone and record retailer Casa Tagini to put together a group in order to record on the Columbia label. There is no documentary evidence to confirm the musicians but they are believed to have been Vicente himself, his brother Domingo on guitar, and Vicente Pecci on flute. Their first recording was the tribute composition by Genaro Vázquez to the tango pianist Rosendo Mendizábal (appropriately entitled *Rosendo*) and on the other side the already long-established *Don Juan* composed by violinist Ernesto Ponzio. The release of the records in 1910 was a significant event in the coming celebration of the bandoneón and tango argentino.

Juan Maglio

In 1880, in the Buenos Aires barrio of Palermo, the Italian immigrant Pantaleón Maglio and his Argentinian wife Carmen became proud parents of Juan Félix (pictured, aged 4). Pantaleón was a player of a simple version of the bandoneón with only 13 buttons, an instrument fast becoming fashionable for playing tango. Whilst growing up, now in the barrio of Boedo, young Juan listened to his father playing at home and was fascinated by his elaborate finger movements. During the day, when

his father was out at work, Juan held the bandoneón and stretched his fingers across the button boards until he was able, gradually, to produce some basic tunes. By 1892 his father was giving his 12-year-old son regular instruction most evenings. In the home his father affectionately called Juan the Italian adjective of *pazzo* or 'crazy boy' and when Juan's friends heard this they nicknamed him the mispronounced 'Pacho'. Pacho the tango bandoneonist became one of the most successful tango giants in the years 1910 to 1920.

At the age of 18 Juan Maglio, who had already been working for almost 6 years, decided that he would prefer to make his living as a musician and so sought more technical tuition. He found a younger but much more experienced and capable bandoneonist called Domingo Santa Cruz[99].

The next year, in 1899, he teamed up with guitarist Luciano Ríos and with the violinist Julián Urdapilleta. Julián's local café was El Vasco in the barrio of Barracas and was where he managed to get the new trio a 3 month contract. By 1904 Juan Maglio was already leading a successful quartet (with the additional member being a flautist) performing across the city and touring the provinces. In 1906 (whilst on separate tours) Maglio and Francisco Canaro met and the latter described Maglio's main feature as a magnificently groomed moustache trained with a leather protector to maintain its shape. For many years afterwards photographs confirm Maglio's fondness for the moustache.

1915
Maglio at home with his wife Teresa

[99] see below in this section

In 1909 Maglio was performing for customers in his local barbershop, Don Leonardo's. We should pause to imagine the scene - here was an already established tango star who had been performing and touring for the previous decade now playing for a small group of men who were either having their hair cut or waiting to do so. This was not a big night out, there was no dancing involved, and the financial reward for Maglio was probably negligible. However, there he was when a young boy entered, as he had done several times before, to listen to and watch the famous 'Pacho'. Until he had heard the alluring sound of the bandoneón from the barbershop that young boy had no interest in music despite the fact that (or maybe because of it) his sister played the piano at home. The 14-year-old had repeatedly asked Maglio for lessons until eventually he agreed, pointing out that he could teach him how to play the instrument but could not teach him how to read music. After only a few months his student, Manuel Pizarro, was good enough to entertain the barber's customers himself and he sought his musical theory education from Carlos Hernani Macchi[100] (who helped many of the tango pioneers in that way). Manuel Pizarro went on to achieve tango fame in Europe from the 1920s until he died in France in 1982[101].

From the 1910s Juan Maglio went from strength to strength and become a top selling tango recording artist and bearer of the title 'The King of Tango'.

---

[100] See *Get To Know the Tango Pioneers 1910 to 1919*

[101] See *Get To Know the Tango Pioneers 1920 to 1935*

Sebastián Ramos Mejia

Sebastián Ramos Mejia was a ticket collector on the horse-drawn streetcars but his passion was the bandoneón. As a skilled, self-taught player he performed in the evenings at local bars and cafés where he was known as El Pardo, referencing his dark skin. As a great enthusiast of the instrument he foresaw its acceptance in to the mainstream music of Buenos Aires telling guitarist/violinist Eusebio Aspiazú in 1883 that the bandoneón would become accepted as a proper instrument and would one day be played at the Teatro Colon[102]. In the 1890s he expanded his enthusiastic reach to bandoneón students by offering lessons via a mail correspondence course, demonstrating that the demand was substantial and widespread. He further encouraged musicians of other instruments to learn the bandoneón and in the following decades he ran his own school not only teaching beginners (such as Vicente Greco and Augusto Berto) but also improving the technique of his more experienced bandoneonist peers such as Antonio Chiappe, José Arturo Severino, Pablo Romero, Domingo Repetto, Antonio Solari and many others.

We will hear no more about Sebastián Ramos Mejía, particularly as he left us neither recordings nor known compositions, but we can acknowledge the influence that he had on others that did. In 1964 the tango lyricist Enrique Cadícamo paid tribute to him with his poem that described him (respectfully but not accurately) as 'the first bandoneonist: El Pardo Sebastián Ramos Mejía'.

---

102 meaning the theatre in the Plaza de Mayo that preceded the current opera house opened in 1908

Domingo Santa Cruz

Domingo Santa Cruz was born in 1884 and his brother Juan in 1885. The boys grew up listening to their father, José Santa Cruz, playing the bandoneón and under his guidance they too became musicians: Domingo a bandoneonist and Juan a guitarist and later pianist. Their father had long been an accomplished player of the concertina and had managed to get hold of a new variant of the instrument - it was rectangular and had buttons at either end producing 34 tones. He would not have known it at the time but he had a hybrid model that fell somewhere between Uhlig's, Zimmerman's, and Band's modifications of the concertina that ultimately led to the bandoneón. With this instrument he played the popular tunes of the day: polkas, mazurkas, habaneras, milongas, and tangos.

In 1899 the brothers Domingo and Juan played as a duet in cafés, bars, and dance salons in the barrios of Almagro, Barracas, La Boca, and Villa Crespo. Domingo became known for his rapid finger movements and dexterity, with each hand playing different runs and variations. Even at such a young age he was sought out as a teacher of this new instrument and taught and guided other pioneers such as Juan Maglio and Vicente Greco. The bandoneonist Vicente Loduca in 1913 described Domingo Santa Cruz as not only one of the first tango bandoneonists but also the best player of all.

Domingo Santa Cruz also composed tangos but, as he could neither read nor write musical notation, he relied on his friend and tango composer Alfredo Bevilacqua to transcribe his music for him. The most familiar of his compositions that is still heard today is *Unión Cívica*, published in 1904. It was first recorded by Juan Maglio in 1912 on the Columbia label but today we know this tango from the versions of Juan D'Arienzo (1938), Rodolfo Biagi (1938), and Osvaldo Pugliese (1958). The sheet music for *Unión Cívica* is marked as a dedication to the local leader of the political party Unión Civica, Manuel J Aparacio, whose power base was in the barrio of Almagro - the area in which Santa Cruz was raised. Such dedications were a common technique to gain patronage for the music, a few pesos, and wider recognition.

Others

We know a little about other bandoneón players on the scene in the period up to 1909 such as:

- Antonio Francisco Chiappe a self-proclaimed talent who placed advertisements in the local newspapers challenging anyone to play better valses than him. He also led a quintet with violin, flute, clarinet, and guitar. Despite his skills, his passion for the instrument, and his local following he chose to dedicate his working life not to music but to the honourable profession of cart driver;

- the butcher, Domingo Cichitti, was well regarded locally as a bandoneón entertainer and gave lessons to increasing numbers of new and ambitious tango musicians;

- 'El Yepi' José María Bianchi was an early source of disappointment to his music teacher, José Guiseppe De Caro De Sica, who was committed to teaching and promoting the finest classical music. Bianchi abandoned his studies to not only play tango but, even worse in De Caro's opinion, on the dreaded bandoneón. De Caro De Sica later lost his own sons (Julio, Francisco, and Emilio De Caro) to the world of tango.

Other frequently repeated names of early bandoneonists include, Nicolas Marmón, 'El Lombardo' Magginini, Domingo Repetto, Sebastián Vázques, Mazuchelli, and Zambrano.

9. Violinists

Casimiro Alcorta

Casimiro Alcorta was a violinist and a composer. He was well-known and admired at the dance halls of the city centre but he was not one of those tango musicians that dressed in refined clothes to ease his way in to the upper-class venues. His violin is said to have been his personification: physically dilapidated with a patchwork of repairs but nevertheless induced energised dancing. His exciting style of unconventionally scratching and plucking the violin strings was adopted by Ernesto Ponzio and later by Edgardo Donato amongst many others. However today he is not particularly remembered for his violin performances but for his unpublished compositions and his lifestyle. His best-known compositions were:

- *Concha sucia* (Dirty shell) that has subsequently attracted a certain infamy due entirely to its implied lewd title. Several versions of added lyrics have emerged over time but we do not what words, if any, were sung whilst Casimiro played it. The tune itself is likely to have been adapted from an earlier traditional melody that can also be heard in Gabino Ezeiza's (pre-1900) composition *Saludo a Paysandu*. The title of *Concha sucia* was changed some time after 1910 to the more socially acceptable *Cara sucia* (Dirty face) and different versions of sanitised lyrics were added - including by Ángel Villoldo who performed it in 1915. Francisco Canaro published the music to *Cara sucia* in 1916 marking it 'arranged by F. Canaro' - he did not claim to be the composer but with the passage of time has frequently become credited as such [103]. Canaro

[103] on 15 September 1928 *Caras y Caretas* published an interview with Francisco Canaro headed 'the author of *Cara sucia*'. Canaro recalled that he was taken to the law courts accused of plagiarism but the court decided in his favour. He made no mention of Casimiro Alcorta.

recorded *Cara sucia* in 1919 with singer Lola Membrives delivering the sweeter lyrics written by Juan Caruso[104]. You can compare and enjoy the *Concha Sucia* melody with that of *Saludo a Paysandu* and a *Cara sucia* version by Canaro (see page 113 Gabino Ezeiza). In 1917 the orquesta típica of Vicente Loduca recorded an instrumental version that has the most playful surges of energy and pizzicato violin.

- *La yapa* meant a 'bonus' that Alcorta always played at the end of his performance - its intended meaning was 'now is the time to put a few pesos in my jar as a gratuity'. Once again Alcorta did not bother to have his music committed to paper nor to register it as his own composition. The melody emerged in 1916 as the tango *Entrada prohibida,* registered and published by flautist Luis Teisseire. We know that tango now by the later versions of Francisco Canaro (1927, 1938), Osvaldo Pugliese (1947), and Juan D'Arienzo (1971). Teisseire was one of many about whom one could say, kindly, rescued old tango tunes, modernised them, committed them to musical notation and published them for wider enjoyment over a longer period.

Casimiro Alcorta lived and worked in the area around the Calle Corrientes – the city's epicentre of theatres and dance halls. In tango history books that area of Buenos Aires is often also labelled as being a centre for prostitutes (which is not an unusual phenomenon in any city in any country in any era) and dance hall

---

[104] although today Canaro's most familiar version is with singer Roberto Maida in 1937

venues are often incorrectly described as brothels. The women working there, whether dancers or hostesses, are indiscriminately labelled as prostitutes and often the resident tango musicians as pimps controlling those women[105]. Such generalisations have clearly produced good reading and created enduring myths but they cannot accurately reflect the variety of circumstances of individual lives, values, and lifestyle choices and so we should read such broad descriptions cautiously and cynically. Casimiro Alcorta, whilst performing at the dance hall Scudo d'Italia, on the street of Corrientes, met and fell in love with the blonde Italian dancer Paulina. Each have casually been categorised as pimp and prostitute yet they lived together as a loving couple and it was in her comforting arms that he passed away in 1913.

Francisco Canaro

The 18-year-old Francisco Canarozzo arrived in Argentina from Italy in 1869 and within a couple of years found himself pulling a handcart of dead porteños, victims of the yellow fever outbreak concentrated around the port barrios of La Boca and San Telmo[106]. Understandably he soon left the city and crossed the Río de la Plata to Uruguay. There he met another Italian immigrant, Rafaela Gatto, married her and started a family. As well as working hard during the day at the local cemetery and in the evenings lighting the street lamps, Francisco Canarozzo became politically active. As a fervent supporter of the movement known as the Colorados he found himself on the wrong side when in 1897 his opponents, the Blancos, gained political control. He fled with his wife, their two daughters Juana and Rosa, and four sons:

---

[105] lunfardo (slang) terms used were *cafishio* and *canfinflero* that can mean 'exploiter of women' but were also words used in a more general and endearing way to mean 'rascal' or 'socially irresponsible'

[106] the fever had started in the north first affecting Paraquay, Brazil and the Argentinian city of Corrientes.

Francisco aged 10, Rafael 8, Juan 6, and Humberto only 2. At some point around that time the family name shortened from Canarozzo to Canaro.

The eldest son Francisco wanted to play a musical instrument but, not being able to afford one, a friend helped him to convert a disused olive oil can in to a violin. That was the start of an extraordinary musical career that endured until the early 1960s.

By 1904 Francisco Canaro junior, aged 16, had learnt to play his first tango - *El Lloron* - but that limited repertoire was not going to help to feed the family. To support his parents and siblings he started to work as a painter preparing the walls, doors and window frames of the (soon to be opened) Congress building. It was there that he met fellow painter and bandoneonist Augusto Berto. Having made a little spare money Canaro bought himself a proper violin and in 1906 he ventured on a tour of the Province of Buenos Aires with his childhood friends, guitarist Rodolfo Duclos [107] and mandolin player Martin Arrevillaga. One of their stops was at Estación de Ranchos and an incident there gives us a feel for the era. Inside, the trio were performing on a raised platform high to the ceiling and outside armed police controlled the entrance. Whilst the trio played they heard shots fired and several bullets ripped through the floor of their stage and continued up in to the ceiling. They narrowly escaped serious injury but unfortunately two policemen did not. Naturally Canaro and his friends wanted to cancel their contract but the café owner gave them assurances, not that it would not happen again but that he would reinforce their

F. CANARO

[107] Duclós later changed his instrument to double bass and can be heard on all of the D'Arienzo recordings from 1935 to 1939.

performance area with iron sheets.

It was during that time in 1906 that Canaro started his studies to read and write musical notation that enabled his rapid growth as a tango composer. He became one of the most successful orchestra leaders, composers, and recording stars all the way up to 1964 and it is reasonably safe to say that his recordings are still heard at least once at every tango dance event around the world today.

Ernesto Ponzio

In the 1880s Carmelo Ponzio was a professional classical harpist and his brother Vicente a violinist whose musical preference was leaning towards the lively sound of tango. In 1885 Carmelo's wife gave birth to a son, Ernesto, and Carmelo was determined to give him the best musical education. Within not too many years he committed to paying for Ernesto to attend a renowned music academy. One night whilst Carmelo was playing on stage he stopped suddenly, fell, and died. Amidst all of the other domestic trauma his widow was unable to maintain the necessary payments for Ernesto's education and so he, not yet 10 years old, had to find work to bring in money for the family. Fortunately for Ernesto his uncle Vicente stepped in to help with an informal musical education and inspired him with enthusiastic tangos on the violin. At the age of 11 Ernesto was energetically busking outside the market at Abasto to earn a few pesos. By the age of 14 the violinist Ernesto was known, unimaginatively, as El Pibe (the Kid) - a name by which he was always known, with a greater degree of imagination, for the rest of his life.

El Pibe was such a talent that tango violinist Genaro Luis Vázquez invited him in to his trio with flautist Luis Teisseire where they played at venues such as El Tambito and other dance clubs. It was during that year at the club Lo de Mamitas that Ernesto is said to have heard the resident pianist Sergio Mendizábal[108] playing an unidentified tango that inspired him in 1900 to 'compose' the tango *Don Juan*. In all likelihood that particular melody played by Sergio was itself a common riff that had already appeared in many improvised country tunes, for example it can be most clearly heard in the anonymous[109] earlier composition *Qué polvo con tanto viento*. Ponzio first named his version *El Panzudo* in tribute to the owner of a bar that he frequently visited but later changed it to *Don Juan* after Don Juan Cabello a well-known porteño in the Palermo night scene. *Don Juan* has the distinction of several firsts in the history of tango: it was on the first record by the first Orquesta Típica Criolla in 1909 and it was performed by Ponzio himself in the first Argentinian feature film with sound *Tango!* in 1933. Today we know *Don Juan* best through the later recordings by Francisco Canaro (1929, 1947, 1959), the Orquesta Típica Victor (1932), Juan D'Arienzo (1936, 1948, 1950), Carlos Di Sarli (1941, 1951, 1955), Roberto Firpo (1951), and many more.

Also in (about) 1900 Ponzio 'composed' the tango *Ataniche*[110] the melody of which is also believed to derive from a now unknown traditional country tune. Today we know *Ataniche* best from the recordings by Juan D'Arienzo (1936) and Roberto Firpo (1942). In 1914 Roberto Firpo recorded (on the Odeon label) *Los Guevara* that had the same, unmistakeable, melody of *Ataniche*.

Ernesto's popularity was increasing rapidly, he was never short of work and moved from one successful group to another. His exuberance whilst playing the violin was described by payador Gabino Ezeiza as generating sparks from his strings, his whole body energised with shoulders rising and falling as if the sounds of the violin were escaping from within deep inside. It is not difficult

---

108 brother of Rosendo, see *Pianists* section above

109 now credited to guitarist Pedro Mansilla Quijano

110 a slang contortion of 'Che, Anita'

to imagine the excitement he generated with his physical energy, his edgy pizzicato plucking and scraping of the violin strings, and his 'tangofication' of already well-loved melodies.

In 1901 he was supporting pianist Alfredo Bevilacqua; in 1902 he was in a trio with flautist Luis Teissere; and in 1903 having returned from a tour with Eusebio Aspiazú he joined a quartet playing second violin to his uncle Vicente, alongside clarinettist Juan Carlos Bazán and harpist 'El Tano' Tortorelli. That quartet played in all of the usual tango venues and dance halls that included Lo de Laura, Lo de Mamita, and Lo de María Vasca. Between 1904 and 1907 Ponzio returned to El Tambito together with Aspiazú and Bazán, sometimes with a changing line-up to include the bandoneón of 'El Yepi' José María Bianchi.

In 1905 Ernesto's good friend the tango flautist Vicente Pecci asked him to be godfather to his son Juan and in due course Ernesto taught young Juan how to play violin in the famous Ponzio style. The enthused and well-trained Juan Pecci went on to spend some 25 years playing tangos in Paris with orchestra leader Eduardo Bianco.

There are several accounts of Ernesto Ponzio becoming argumentative during his performances. In about 1904 at the dance hall Milonga de Pantaleon he became involved in a fight and was injured resulting in a short break from performing. His increasingly aggressive outbursts started to become a common feature over the following years resulting in him being arrested several times for brawling until in 1924 his temper culminated in shooting a man dead.

Flautists

Vicente Pecci

Vicente Pecci was born in Italy in 1886 and by the age of 13 he was in Buenos Aires and playing flute alongside guitarist Eusebio Aspiazú. That same year he was playing tangos with pianist Enrique Saborido and violinist Genaro Vázquez and in 1900 he was accompanying the energetic violinist Ernesto Ponzio with whom he became a close friend.

In 1903 he was in a quartet with Ponzio, clarinetist Juan Carlos Bazán, and the harpist Tortorelli. They played at many of the most popular venues of the day but it was during that tour that Ponzio was injured in a brawl, bringing the quartet to an end.

Vicente Pecci was popular amongst his fellow tango musicians and played alongside the emerging stars of the bandoneón, the instrument that would prompt the gradual disappearance of his instrument from the orquesta típica. Despite the flute's imminent redundancy Pecci remained a much sought-after addition to the orquesta típica line-up. From 1909 until about 1919 his flute can be heard on recordings by the orquestas típicas of Vicente Greco, Genaro Esposito, and Eduardo Arolas.

Luis Teisseire

The life of Luis Teisseire changed direction when he was the recipient of a gifted flute.

He was born in 1883 to a French father and Italian mother who had wanted him to become a doctor but when his father had a serious accident Luis abandoned his studies in order to find work. During his teenage years he witnessed the mistreatment of employees leading him to become active in pursuit of the, as yet non-existent, rights of the working man. He joined the growing anarchist movement, led industrial strikes, and frequently found himself dismissed by his various employers.

In 1900, aged 18, Luis Teisseire was dreaming of studying music and becoming a violinist whilst in reality he was selling newspapers on the streets. He discovered that one of the other boys alongside him was illiterate. Luis was dismayed by yet another example of the exploitative system that could produce a worker unable to benefit from the product that he was selling. Luis taught the boy to read and in return the boy (knowing the unfulfilled dreams of Luis to become a musician) unexpectedly rewarded him with a flute with the condition that Luis had to learn how to play. By the end of the year Luis Teisseire was accompanying other musicians at cafés and dance halls in La Boca, Palermo, and Retiro. In 1901 the violinist Genaro Vázquez and the blind guitarist/violinist Eusebio Aspiazú invited him to form a trio. Teisseire improved rapidly and widened his musical prowess to such an extent that at the 1907 February carnival he participated in a performance of a choral group consisting of an unimaginable 300 singers.

Sr. LUIS TEISSEIRE

In 1911 he performed his successful 1909 tango composition in a trio at the Bar Exposición where the owner successfully petitioned him to dedicate the tango to his bar. The subsequent record labels bore both titles *Cosa linda, barata / Bar Exposición.* In 1912 Teisseire teamed up with bandoneonist Augusto Berto to play at the famous Bar Domínguez and in 1913 was in the Augusto Berto Quintet when they recorded on the Atlantic Record label.

Ironically it was the bandoneón that led to the redundancy of the flute and so Teisseire focused on composing (tangos and other musical genre) and enjoyed prolonged success in theatre productions. His compositions were many, and successful, but are largely unknown to us today - as many fine tangos are - because they by chance were not recorded by those few orchestras in the 1930s and 1940s that provide the majority of the dance music heard at today's milongas.

The most familiar are:

- *Bar Exposición* (first entitled *Casa linda, barata* in 1909) thanks to the later recordings by Francisco Canaro (1932), Carlos Di Sarli (1943, 1952, and 1954), and Rodolfo Biagi (1961); and
- *Entrada prohibida* recorded by Francisco Canaro (1927, 1938), and Osvaldo Pugliese (1947).

11. Guitarists

There was no shortage of capable guitarists and nearly all duos, trios, and quartets included the guitar as the provider of chord accompaniment, bass runs, and percussion. In the above sections we have heard briefly about:

- Luciano Ríos the regular guitarist with bandoneonist Juan Maglio as well as playing with Eduardo Arolas and Domingo Santa Cruz;
- Rodolfo Duclos who played with violinist Francisco Canaro. Duclos wrote the music and lyrics to a vals *Recuerdos de la pampa* that was recorded by Juan D'Arienzo (1939);
- three guitarists who each played together with their bandoneonist brothers: Luis Bernstein (with Arturo); Domingo Greco (with Vicente), and Juan Santa Cruz (with Domingo);
- Luis Bernstein was also a composer of tangos, several of which we hear today thanks to the recordings of others

Composition	Best Known Recordings
Don Goyo	Juan D'Arienzo (1946, 1957)
El abrojito	Osvaldo Pugliese (1945)
Pa'que llorar	Orquesta Típica Victor (1927)

- Ricardo González played guitar and taught it to Eduardo Arolas. Amongst his compositions was the tango *La Rosarina* subsequently recorded by the Orquest Típica Victor (1929), Juan D'Arienzo (1937), Roberto Firpo (1936, 1944, 1949) and Francisco Canaro (1943);
- Félix Camarano who played with bandoneonist Genaro Espósito.

We will finish with a brief look at a popular guitarist who remains the quintessence of the early tango scene.

Eusebio Aspiazú

In July 1879 Eusebio Aspiazú was with his mother in the city centre watching the celebrations of Argentina's Declaration of Independence when, during the firework display, a projectile flew out of control and hit him in the face. At 14 years old Eusebio was blinded in both eyes. With his options for work severely limited he learnt to play guitar and in 1883 joined a trio by providing both a percussive strum and the full range of powerful bass notes, on guitars sometimes with nine and eleven strings. By 1889 he had accompanied (at different times) the celebrated payador Pablo Vázquez and the established tango musicians: violinist Ernesto Ponzio, bandoneonists Antonio Chiappe and Sebastián Ramos Mejía, and flautists Vicente Pecci and Luis Teisseire.

The census of 1895 gives us a glimpse of the private life of Aspiazú. He is shown as 29 years old, married in 1887, employed as a musician, blind, and illiterate. His wife, Lastenia, was a literate ironing lady with five children only four of whom were listed as living with them: Francisco (aged 7 who was already attending school and able to read and write) and three daughters Modesta (4), Lastenia (3), and Delia (2).

In 1901 Aspiazú was the guitarist in a trio with Roque Rinaldi (violin) and Vicente Pecci (flute) at the late-night bar El Tambito in the park of Palermo. As usual, customers were making requests for tunes but one particularly noisy customer, Juan Carlos Argerich from a rich and powerful family, demanded that they play a tango that the trio either did not know or refused to play. The story is that, frustrated and presumably drunk, Argerich threw his drink at them, then his glass, followed by a bottle. In the uproar he wielded a chair threatening everybody and in the ensuing struggle Argerich was stabbed in the abdomen, fatally. The killer was a gangster whose good connections with his local political leader ensured that he served a token two years in prison. A couple of decades later that gangster became good friends with, and underworld protector of, the folk and tango singer Carlos Gardel.

After 1910 there is little known about Aspiazú. However at the age of 63 he returned to the front line of tango (in 1928) when he joined up with two former friends, violinist Ernesto Ponzio and clarinettist Juan Carlos Bazán, together with fellow veterans the pianist Enrique Saborido, violinist Alcides Palavecino, and flautist Vicente Pecci. They formed the Orquesta Típica de la Guardia Vieja (a retrospective tribute to the old days) and performed to rapturous receptions for the following 5 years.

Eusebio Aspiazú lived to a respectable 80 years old, passing away in 1945.

The Continuing Story

As you have seen, there was a vibrant tango scene in live performances and recordings in the years up to 1909. It was the environment in which future tango stars were growing up and absorbing the culture around them.

The story of tango and its pioneers continues in the series *Get To Know the Tango Pioneers* with linked on-line music tracks and film clips:

Celebration of Tango Argentino: 1910 to 1919

includes the creation, recording, and celebration of the orquesta típica; the arrival of the cabarets; the proliferation of tango recordings; and the start of the tango film industry. We also see the appearance of names that are familiar to today's tango fans, including: Ángel D'Agostino, Juan D'Arienzo, Julio De Caro, Enrique Delfino, Carlos Di Sarli, Osvaldo Fresedo, Carlos Gardel, and Francisco Lomuto.

The Precarious Years: 1920 to 1935

includes the growth of tango in recordings, the theatre, films with sound, and the new technological reach of radio. We also see the emergence of poets and singers, and of musicians and orchestra leaders that are familiar to today's tango fans, including: Rodolfo Biagi, Miguel Caló, Lucio Demare, Edgardo Donato, Pedro Laurenz, Osvaldo Pugliese, Ricardo Tanturi, and Aníbal Troilo.

Bandoneón: a musical instrument, like a concertina, with buttons rather than piano keys and is almost exclusively associated with tango
Barrio: an area in a city, often with a distinct characteristic
Candombe: a drum-based rhythm associated with African origin
Compadrito: a young man who is, or is trying to appear, cool
Conventillo: over-crowded social housing with a shared patio space
Corte: a dance move associated with, but preceded, tango
Criollo: creole, of mixed ethnic origin
Gaucho: a non-city dweller elevated by literature to an heroic figure
Gringo: a European immigrant to the Americas
Habanera: music and dance style named after Havana (Cuba) also known as 'tango americano'
Lunfardo: a Buenos Aires slang
Milonga: a national song; a post-1932 dance rhythm; a dance event
Organito: a portable mechanical instrument with bellows
Orquesta Típica: a group of musicians playing tango dance music, with bandoneón
Payador: a singer/guitarist of melancholic, traditionally improvised, verse
Porteño: a resident of Buenos Aires
Quebrada: a dance move associated with, but preceded, tango
Rondalla: a group of musicians playing stringed instruments
Tambor: a drum associated with African heritage; Tambo a meeting place

Tango americano: same as the habanera, definitely not from North America
Tango andaluz: from Southern Spain also called Tango Gitano (Gypsy) and Tango Flamenco
Tango argentino: I use this to denote the musical genre that emerged from Buenos Aires in the early 1900s, distinct from the 2 forms above
Tango canción: a sung tango, not for the dance market
Vals: the Spanish spelling of waltz
Zarzuela: a Spanish theatre play with song and dance, the sainete is a variant as is the revista but is (generally) without music.

The illustrations and photographs have been reproduced with the kind permission of:

Archivo General de la Nación de Argentina, Buenos Aires, Argentina;

Biblioteca Nacional de España, Madrid, Spain;

Ibero-Amerikanisches Institut, Berlin, Germany;

author photograph (p183) and cover artwork courtesy of Adrian Cubitt;

other images are sourced from material in the Public Domain.

Cover illustration published in Buenos Aires 1908.

On-line material includes the complete collection at the:

- Biblioteca Nacional de España, (Hemeroteca Digital);
- Ibero-Amerikanisches Institut;
- Discography of American Historical Recordings;
- UCSB Cylinder Audio Archive;
- Library of Congress; and the
- Archivo General de la Nación de Argentina.

A multitude of other websites have provided access to newspapers, magazines, photographs, record labels, discographies, recordings, population census, genealogy, travel and migration information.

Published works include:

- A city of trades: Spanish and Italian Immigrants in Late 19th Century Buenos Aires (for the European Historical Economics Society) *Blanca Sánchez-Alonso*
- Argentina 1516-1987 *David Rock*
- Between the Gaucho and the Tango…1895–1915 *Brian Bockelman*
- Blackness and Urban Popular Sectors in Buenos Aires (1895-1916) *Lea Geler*
- Buenos Aires: Arrabal-Sainete-Tango, *Domingo Casadevall*
- Buenos Aires Setenta Años Atrás *Dr. José Antonio Wilde*
- Carlos Gardel *Simon Collier*
- Cine Argentino *Octavio Getin,*
- Cosas de negros *Vicente Rossi*
- Doce Ventanas del Tango *Fundación El Libro*
- El Arte del Payador *Raúl Dorra*
- El Encanto de Buenos Aires *Gómez Carillo*
- El tango argentino como espejo de la sociedad en su

contexto histórico *Professor Dr. Christian Wentzlaff-Eggebert*

- El Tango Argentino de Salon *Nicanor Lima*
- El Tango en la sociedad porteña 1880-1920 *Hugo Lamas & Enrique Binda*
- El Tango en Mis Recuerdos *Julio De Caro*
- El Tango su Historia y Evolución *Horacio Ferrer*
- En Argentine de Buenos Aires au Gran Chaco *Jules Huret*
- Entre Cortes y Quebradas, Candombes, Milongas, y Tangos en su Historia y Comentarios *Pintín Castellanos*
- Entre fonógrafos y radios: difusión del tango durante las primeras décadas del siglo XX *Andrea Matallana*
- Evaristo Carriego *Jorge Luis Borges*
- Fábricas de Músicas *Marina Cañardo*
- Folklore en el Uruguay, La Guitarra del Gaucho, Sus Danzas y Canciones *Cedar Viglietti*
- Herencia Africana en el Tango 1870-1890 *Gustavo Goldman*
- Immigrants in the Lands of Promise: Italians in Buenos Aires and New York. *Samuel L. Baily*
- La Historia de la Orquesta Típica *Luis Adolfo Sierra*
- La Historia del Tango Volumes 1 to 18 *published by Corregidor*
- La música en los inicios del cine sonoro argentino *Rosa Chalkho*
- Las Raices del Tango *Eduardo Giorlandini*
- Lo Criollo en el Tango *Susana Ibarburu*
- Los Primeros 25 Años de la Fonográfia Argentina *Enrique Binda*
- Mis Memorias *Francisco Canaro*
- Music Trade Review magazines 1905 - 1928
- Nueva Historia del Tango *Héctor Benedetti*
- Otros tangos origenes mediaticos del tango en el teatro y

la danza *Jimena Anabel Jauregui,*

- Popular, Elite and Mass Culture The Spanish Zarzuela in Buenos Aires 1890-1900 *Kristen McCleary*
- Recording Studios on Tour: The Expeditions of the Victor Talking Machine Company through Latin America 1903-1926, a dissertation by *Sergio Daniel Ospina Romero*
- Sainete y cine sonoro argentino *Alicia Aisemberg*
- Talking Machine Review magazines 1905-1927
- Tango Testigo Social *Andrés Carretero*
- Tango Aborigen *Marisa Uthurralt & Alberto González Arzac*
- The Afro-Argentines of Buenos Aires 1800-1900 *George Reid Andrews*
- The Argentina Reader *published by Gabriela Nouzeilles & Graciela Montaldo*
- The Art History of Love *Robert Farris Thompson*
- The Invention of Argentina *Nicolas Shunway*
- The Quest for the Embrace *Gustavo Benzecry Sabá*
- The Zonophone Record 1901-1903 *Ernie Bayly & Michael Kinnear*

Additionally I have researched several hundred book extracts, academic papers, opinion pieces, articles, interviews, letters, and collations of multiple sources and so I apologise for the inevitable omission from the above list of other contributing information.

Index

David's research in to the history of Argentine tango precedes the authorship of this book by over a decade, and continues today. His investigative methods draw on his professional background: for over 30 years David served in several UK national intelligence and investigation agencies. He enjoys applying his skills (securing multiple corroborative sources to identify people, their associates, and their activities) to the more cultural world of tango.

More recently (2021/2022) David completed a Diploma course (*La Historia del Tango*) with the Instituto Argentino del Tango, Buenos Aires, Argentina.

David presents seminars on *Get To Know the Tango Orchestras* and *Get To Know the Tango Pioneers*. He enjoys dancing tango, is a tango DJ and (with his wife Marion) organises milongas and tango classes. At time of publication he is also Chairman of the UK Argentine Tango Association.

Printed in Dunstable, United Kingdom

70796011R00107